Life on the Lines: Aisha's

Table of Contents

1. Chapter One – Empty Spaces

2. Chapter Two – The Care Home

3. Chapter Three – New Girls, New Games

4. Chapter Four – First Favour

5. Chapter Five – Mel

6. Chapter Six – Shifts and Shadows

7. Chapter Seven – Under Pressure

8. Chapter Eight – The Setup

9. Chapter Nine – The Beating

10. Chapter Ten – Fallout

11. Chapter Eleven – YS's History

12. Chapter Twelve – Unspoken Warnings

13. Chapter Thirteen – Slipping Further
14. Chapter Fourteen – Something's Off
15. Chapter Fifteen – The Betrayal
16. Chapter Sixteen – Silent Confessions
17. Chapter Seventeen – Lost Control
18. Chapter Eighteen – Trauma Bonds
19. Chapter Nineteen – YS's Reign
20. Chapter Twenty – Addiction and Obsession
21. Chapter Twenty-One – Broken Dreams
22. Chapter Twenty-Two – Shante's Fall
23. Chapter Twenty-Three – Kyle's Regret
24. Chapter Twenty-Four – Close Encounters
25. Chapter Twenty-Five – Power Plays
26. Chapter Twenty-Six – Darkness at the Door
27. Chapter Twenty-Seven – The Warehouse
28. Chapter Twenty-Eight – Spiralling

29. Chapter Twenty-Nine – Boiling Point

30. Chapter Thirty – No More Games

31. Chapter Thirty-One – Blood and Silence

32. Chapter Thirty-Two – The Breaking

33. Chapter Thirty-Three – The Cost

34. Chapter Thirty-Four – Numb

35. Chapter Thirty-Five – Kyle's Confession

36. Chapter Thirty-Six – Wounds that Don't Heal

37. Chapter Thirty-Seven – Dying Light

38. Chapter Thirty-Eight – Collision

39. Chapter Thirty-Nine – Consequences

40. Chapter Forty – Aftermath

41. Chapter Forty-One – The Edge

42. Chapter Forty-Two – The Waiting Room

43. Chapter Forty-Three – The Fall of YS

44. Chapter Forty-Four – Holding On

45. Chapter Forty-Five – Cracks Beneath the Surface

46. Chapter Forty-Six – In the Dark

47. Chapter Forty-Seven – Broken Bargains

48. Chapter Forty-Eight – Ghosts in Her Blood

49. Chapter Forty-Nine – Lines Still Crossed

50. Chapter Fifty – Missing Pieces

51. Final Chapter – A Message

Chapter 1: The Beginning of the End

Aisha had never felt truly alone before. Not like this. Not until the day she was placed in the children's residential home after her mum died.

The house smelled of cheap air freshener and something deeper, something stale—like too many lives had passed through, leaving behind ghosts of the ones who never made it out.

She had no family to take her in. No one had stepped forward. No one had claimed her.

She was fourteen and completely alone.

The weight of it pressed against her chest, suffocating her in ways she didn't know how to describe. No one had told her how grief could feel so physical, how it could make her limbs heavy, her stomach tight, her throat dry.

The silence in her new room was unbearable. It wasn't the comforting quiet of home, where she used to listen to her mum humming while she cooked, or the sound of

Darnell's music playing too loud in the next room. This was a different kind of silence—empty, hollow. The kind that made her feel like she didn't exist.

She lay on the thin mattress, staring at the ceiling, willing herself not to cry. She had cried enough. First when Darnell died, then when her mum couldn't cope, and then when her mum was gone too. Now? Now she felt numb.

Her fingers curled around the duvet, gripping it tight as if that would ground her, keep her from falling into the abyss that had been threatening to swallow her whole since she lost them both.

What had she done to deserve this?

Her mum had tried. Aisha knew that. But after Darnell was killed, it was like something inside her just… broke. She stopped eating properly. Stopped sleeping. Stopped being the mum Aisha knew. The grief consumed her, ate away at her until there was nothing left.

Aisha had spent so many nights listening to her cry through the walls, feeling helpless, terrified. She had tried to hold things together, tried to be strong. But in the end, it hadn't been enough. Her mum had wasted away in front of her, her body shutting down as if it just couldn't bear to keep going without Darnell.

And now, Aisha was here. Alone. Forgotten.

She barely spoke to the staff, barely acknowledged the other girls. But one of them didn't take the hint.

Kellie.

Sixteen, loud, confident in a way Aisha wasn't. She had a sharp laugh and a sharper tongue, her presence filling the space like she belonged there, like she had nothing to be afraid of. She spoke to the care home staff like they were beneath her, rolling her eyes at their instructions, mocking them behind their backs. There was something about the way she moved, the way she took up space like the world owed her something, that intrigued Aisha.

Kellie was everything Aisha wasn't—bold, brash, untouchable. And she noticed Aisha in a way no one else had.

Aisha had expected to be invisible in this place. She had wanted to be. But Kellie wouldn't let that happen.

"You look like you hate it here more than I do," Kellie said, flopping onto the seat next to Aisha at breakfast one morning. Her tone was teasing, but there was an edge to it, like she knew exactly how Aisha was feeling.

Aisha hesitated, unsure of how to respond. She didn't hate it here. She didn't feel anything at all. But Kellie wasn't waiting for an answer.

"You should come out with me sometime," she said. "Get out of this shithole for a bit."

Aisha looked at her then, properly. There was something unreadable in Kellie's expression, like she was testing her. Aisha should have said no. But instead, she nodded.

And that was where it all began.

Chapter 2: The Introduction

It started with small things.

Kellie invited Aisha out, handed her a can of cider, a cigarette. It was easy. It was normal. It was nothing serious.

Then came the shoplifting. The late-night sneaking out. The whispers of something bigger, something that felt like freedom but wasn't.

Kellie introduced her to the crew.

And that was when she met **him**.

YS.

Eighteen, sharp-eyed, always in control. He didn't say much, but when he did, people listened. Aisha listened.

There was something different about YS. He wasn't like the loud, posturing boys she'd seen before, the ones who talked big but never followed through. He had a quiet kind of power, the kind that didn't need to be shouted about. The kind that made people fall in line without him even asking.

People respected YS. They feared him, too, but they never showed it. That was the thing about him—he didn't demand respect. He already had it. And Aisha could feel it the moment she laid eyes on him.

"Who's this?" YS asked, his eyes landing on Aisha. There was something unsettling about the way he looked at her, like he was already figuring her out, already deciding whether she was worth his time.

"This is Aisha," Kellie said, grinning.

"She's cool."

Aisha's stomach twisted, though she wasn't sure why. She nodded at YS, keeping her expression neutral. She didn't want to seem intimidated, even though she was.

YS studied her for a moment before nodding back.

"You roll with Kellie, yeah?"

Aisha hesitated before answering.

"Yeah."

"Cool," he said simply, before turning back to his conversation.

That was it. No big welcome, no dramatic introduction. But something about the exchange stuck with her.

It wasn't just the way he carried himself, the way people seemed to orbit around him. It was the way she suddenly wanted to prove herself. To show him she wasn't just some kid.

She glanced at Kellie, who had straightened up, her usual relaxed stance shifting slightly. Aisha noticed the way Kellie laughed a little louder than before, the way she edged just a bit closer to YS. It was subtle, but Aisha caught it—Kellie was trying to impress him.

Aisha's gaze flickered to another girl in the group, Shante, who had been talking but had suddenly gone quiet. Shante's jaw was tight, her expression unreadable, but Aisha sensed something underneath—the same way she sensed tension in a room before something kicked off.

Kellie barely acknowledged Shante, acting as though she wasn't even there.

And YS? He barely acknowledged either of them, like he already had what he wanted and anything else was just background noise.

Aisha didn't know what that meant yet.

But she would soon enough.

She didn't know it then, but that moment? That first night? It was the beginning of the end.

Chapter 3: The First Favour

It started small.

Aisha was standing with Kellie outside a chicken shop, laughing at something stupid, when YS approached them. He wasn't smiling, but he wasn't cold either. There was something about the way he moved—measured, purposeful. Like everything he did had been decided long before he did it.

"Aisha, yeah?" YS asked, standing in front of her. His presence pulled all the attention onto him, like he was the sun and everyone else was orbiting.

Aisha nodded, feeling a small flicker of nervous energy in her chest. She didn't want to look unsure. Not in front of him.

YS reached into his pocket, pulling out a small package wrapped in cling film. He held it up between his fingers like it weighed nothing. "Hold this for me," he said, his tone casual, like it wasn't even a request.

Aisha hesitated for a second—just a second—before reaching out and taking it. The plastic felt warm in her palm, like it had been sitting in his pocket for a while. She didn't know exactly what was inside, but she wasn't stupid.

YS studied her reaction, his gaze unreadable. "Cool," he said, nodding before turning back to his conversation with someone else.

Just like that, it was done. No explanation. No reassurance. No questions asked.

But Aisha's stomach was flipping.

She had just taken something from YS.

She was holding something for him.

Kellie grinned at her. "See? Told you, you're good."

Aisha tried to smile back, but her mind was racing. Had she just done something illegal? Was this a test? And why did she feel a small rush of pride that YS had trusted her with something?

She told herself it was nothing. Just a favour. Just a small thing.

But deep down, she knew—this was the start of something bigger.

Kellie watched closely, her eyes flicking between Aisha and YS. She had been in this exact position before, the moment where someone was tested for the first time. The difference was, Kellie had known exactly what she was getting into. Aisha, though? She was still innocent in all this.

That was why it was so interesting to watch.

Aisha hesitated, and for a split second, Kellie wondered if she was going to back out. If she did, YS would write her off completely—he didn't have time for dead weight. But then Aisha took the package, and Kellie felt a flicker of satisfaction.

She had chosen right.

Aisha wasn't just some scared little girl. She had something in her. And YS saw it too. That was good.

Right?

Kellie shook the thought away, grinning as she elbowed Aisha. "See? Easy."

But as Aisha's fingers curled tightly around the package, Kellie couldn't ignore the small pang of guilt in her chest.

Aisha could still feel the weight of the package in her hand long after she had shoved it into her jacket pocket. It wasn't heavy, but it may as well have been a brick.

Her heart was racing, and she hated that she didn't know if it was fear or excitement.

She looked at YS, who had already moved on to another conversation, as if nothing had happened. As if she wasn't standing there questioning everything. That was the difference between them, wasn't it?

For YS, this was just another moment. Just another day. But for Aisha, it was the first step into something she wasn't sure she could come back from.

Kellie was watching her, smiling like this was normal. Like this was fun.

Aisha forced herself to breathe.

She wasn't in danger.

She was in control.

Right?

But the longer she stood there, the more she wasn't so sure.

Chapter 4: The Crew

The more time Aisha spent with the crew, the more she started to understand the way things worked.

Kellie was well-liked, but she wasn't in charge. She played her role—keeping girls close, making sure people felt welcome. But YS? YS was different.

Everything revolved around him.

And people like Shante noticed that.

Shante had been around longer than Aisha, and it was obvious she didn't like that Kellie was bringing someone new in. Every time Aisha spoke, Shante watched her like she was trying to figure out what she was about. It made Aisha feel small, like she was still on the outside looking in.

But Kellie? Kellie seemed almost proud to have Aisha with her, like she had brought in something valuable. And Aisha liked that feeling.

Still, she could sense Kellie's need for approval, the way her energy changed around YS. Aisha started noticing the way Kellie laughed a little too hard at his jokes, the way she tried to impress him—standing a little closer, making comments she knew he'd like. It was subtle, but Aisha picked up on it. And she wasn't the only one.

Shante saw it too. She barely acknowledged Kellie, and when she did, it was sharp, passive-aggressive. Aisha wasn't sure what their history was, but there was something unspoken between them—a rivalry that went deeper than just words. Aisha wondered if Kellie noticed, or if she was too focused on making herself stand out to YS.

Kellie knew exactly what she was doing. She had worked hard to earn YS's attention, and she wasn't about to let anyone take her place—not Aisha, and definitely not Shante.

She liked Aisha, but there was an unspoken rule in this life—everyone was replaceable. If Aisha was useful, Kellie would keep her close. If she became a problem, well… Kellie had learned to cut people off before they could do the same to her.

She glanced at Shante, who was watching Aisha with that smug look again. Shante had been around longer, but YS didn't take her seriously. Kellie made sure of that. If Shante thought she could push Aisha out, she had another thing coming.

One night, they were all standing around at a block party, music vibrating through the air, when YS turned to Aisha again.

"You busy?"

Aisha swallowed, shaking her head.

"Cool. Take this to Lamar," he said, handing her something small. "He's by the chicken shop. Tell him it's from me."

Kellie elbowed Aisha, grinning. "Go on, then."

Aisha hesitated. This was different. This wasn't just holding something. This was moving something. Her chest tightened. Was this the line she wasn't meant to cross? But before she could even second-guess herself, Shante scoffed from the side.

"Should've asked someone who knows what they're doing," Shante muttered under her breath.

Kellie's jaw tightened. Shante was testing Aisha, pushing her, trying to see if she'd crumble.

Kellie turned to Aisha, eyes sharp. She needed Aisha to do this, to prove herself. If Aisha hesitated now, she'd always be seen as the weak one, the girl YS let tag along but never took seriously.

Aisha took the package and left.

Kellie exhaled slowly, smirking at Shante. "Guess she knows what she's doing after all."

Shante rolled her eyes but said nothing. Kellie turned back to YS, heart racing. Aisha had passed the test.

And now? Now she was in.

YS watched Aisha as she walked away, his expression unreadable. He had seen this a hundred times before—quiet ones, nervous ones, the ones who hesitated before doing what they were told.

But there was something different about her.

She wasn't just scared. She was thinking. Calculating. Trying to figure out where she stood.

That was good. That meant she had potential.

YS wasn't interested in girls who blindly followed orders. They burned out fast, made mistakes, or crumbled under pressure. Aisha was different. She was hesitant, yes, but that hesitation wasn't weakness—it was strategy. She was measuring up the situation, figuring out what was expected of her before committing.

He liked that.

He leaned back slightly, his gaze shifting to Kellie. He could see how hard she was trying to make this work, to prove she had made the right decision by bringing Aisha in. Kellie was useful, but she was also predictable. She wanted approval, wanted to impress. Aisha, on the other hand, didn't seem like she needed validation. That made her interesting.

Shante's reaction didn't go unnoticed either. YS saw the way she bristled, the way she watched Aisha like she was sizing up competition. That was another advantage—tension like that created control. Shante would work harder to stay in his good books, Kellie would double down to keep Aisha on her side, and Aisha? She was still figuring out her place. He could mold that.

A slow smirk tugged at the corner of his lips. Let them think this was Kellie's project. Let them think Aisha was just another lost girl being brought into the fold.

Soon enough, she'd be his.

Chapter 5: Aisha's Growing Loyalty

Aisha didn't even realise how quickly things changed.

She had a place now. People knew her name. YS acknowledged her in a way he didn't with most girls. Even Kellie looked at her differently—like she had leveled up.

But with that came expectations.

At first, it was small. More favours. More errands. YS would call, and she'd come running. Kellie reassured her that this was normal, that it meant she was trusted. But there were moments, late at night, when Aisha lay in bed staring at the ceiling, and she wasn't sure if this was trust or something else entirely.

She told herself she wasn't scared. But she was.

The care home staff started noticing. They were getting frustrated. Aisha was hardly ever around, and when she was, she had an attitude. The once-quiet girl who kept to herself was now pushing boundaries—staying out late, missing curfews, talking back. The staff didn't know how to handle her. They reported her to Mel.

Mel, her social worker, pulled her aside one day, wearing that fake concerned face Aisha had come to despise. Aisha tensed the moment she saw her, already knowing what was coming.

Aisha didn't like Mel. She was one of those social workers who thought they knew everything about everything just because they'd watched a few Channel 5 documentaries. Truth was, Mel knew f*** all. She was textbook-taught, no real-life experience. Straight out of school, straight to college, then university to study social work. She was one of those who believed that if a girl was going missing, she was automatically involved in CSE, and if a boy sold a bit of weed to his mates, then he was the next Pablo Escobar.

Mel didn't know Aisha. Didn't understand her world. But she still acted like she did. That was what Aisha hated the most—the fake understanding, the soft, concerned voice, like she actually cared.

"Aisha, I need you to be honest with me," Mel started.

"What's been going on?"

Aisha folded her arms.

"Nothing."

Mel sighed, rubbing her forehead.

"Listen, Aisha... I've seen this before. I know what's happening."

"No, you don't," Aisha snapped, her chest tightening. "You don't know anything about me."

Mel held back her frustration. She had been doing this job for a couple of years now, and she genuinely believed she was making a difference. She wanted to help. That was why she got into social work—to save girls like Aisha.

But Aisha wasn't making it easy.

Mel truly believed she could get through to her if she just tried hard enough. If she said the right thing, pushed at the right time, maybe Aisha would let her in.

But the truth was, Aisha didn't trust her. She saw Mel as just another professional who pretended to care, another person in a long list of adults who thought they knew what was best for her.

Mel tried to soften her voice.

"I just want to make sure you're safe, Aisha. That's all."

Aisha rolled her eyes.

"I am safe."

"Are you?" Mel pressed. "Because disappearing for hours, missing curfew, running around with people we don't know—that's not safe."

Aisha's jaw clenched.

"You don't know who I'm with."

Mel gave her a look. "Then tell me."

Silence.

Aisha wasn't stupid.

Mel sighed again. "Just… don't trust people too easily, okay?"

Aisha bit the inside of her cheek to stop herself from snapping back. The irony.

She didn't trust people.

Except maybe YS.

And that was all that mattered.

Mel walked away from the conversation with Aisha feeling defeated.

She had gone into social work to save people—to make a difference. She wasn't stupid. She knew the system was broken, knew how many kids fell through the cracks. But she believed in what she was doing.

She just wished Aisha could see that.

Mel knew Aisha didn't trust her, but that didn't stop her from trying. She had to try. That was her job. That was why she spent hours reading case studies, learning new intervention techniques, trying to build trust with the young people on her caseload.

But Aisha looked at her like she was the enemy. Like she was just another adult trying to control her.

And that stung.

She had been warned that some kids wouldn't want saving. That some of them would push back no matter what you did. But Mel didn't believe that.

She just needed to find the right approach.

She wouldn't give up on Aisha.

Not yet.

Kellie could see the change happening. She had seen it before—how quickly girls got sucked in, how easily they became loyal.

She wasn't sure how she felt about it.

On one hand, Aisha was proving herself, which meant Kellie had been right about her. YS wouldn't have kept her around otherwise. But there was another part of Kellie, a part she didn't like to acknowledge, that felt uneasy.

Because Aisha wasn't just following orders.

She was starting to believe in them.

That was dangerous.

Kellie had been in this life long enough to know that belief was what got you trapped.

And once you were trapped, there was no way out.

YS had seen enough to know that Aisha was going to be useful.

She was smart. Smarter than Kellie gave her credit for. She was still cautious, still weighing up every situation before diving in, but that was a good thing. He needed girls who thought things through, not ones who acted on impulse.

And the best part? She trusted him.

He saw it in the way she reacted when he spoke, in the way she checked her phone every time he messaged. He was in her head now, whether she realised it or not.

And soon, she'd be exactly where he needed her to be.

Chapter 6: Deeper Into the Game

Aisha's life was starting to change, and it was happening fast.

Her phone buzzed constantly—messages from Kellie, from YS, from unknown numbers with instructions that she barely questioned anymore. Aisha had gone from running the odd errand to being involved properly. The thrill, the sense of importance, it was all-consuming.

But beneath it? There was something else. A heaviness that clung to her.

She wasn't sure she liked it.

The care home staff had run out of patience with Aisha. It wasn't just the late nights anymore. It was her whole attitude.

She barely spoke to them unless she had to, and when she did, it was short, clipped, filled with sarcasm. The girl they had once been worried about—because of her grief, her isolation—was now a different kind of worry. She was out of reach.

Karen, one of the senior carers, sighed heavily as she scanned the sign-in sheet. Aisha hadn't signed back in until nearly 3 a.m. the night before. Again.

"She's out of control," Karen muttered to her colleague. "If she keeps this up, she's going to get herself into real trouble."

"She's already in trouble," the other staff member replied. "She just doesn't see it yet."

Karen pursed her lips.

"Well, she better wake up before it's too late."

Aisha could feel their eyes on her when she walked through the kitchen in the mornings. The disapproving stares. The fake, tight-lipped smiles. But she didn't care. She had somewhere else to be now. Someone else to answer to.

And that meant their opinions didn't matter.

What annoyed her most was how predictable they were. The whispered discussions behind her back, the looks they shared when they thought she wasn't paying attention. They saw her as another lost cause, another problem they had to deal with.

They didn't understand. They never would.

Mel felt like she was failing.

She had tried everything—calm conversations, warnings, even veiled threats about what could happen if Aisha wasn't careful. Nothing worked.

And the worst part? Aisha wasn't scared.

Mel had worked with enough young people to know the ones who were close to the edge. Aisha was one of them.

One wrong move. One bad situation. And she'd be lost to this world completely.

She watched Aisha scroll through her phone during another tense meeting, pretending like she wasn't listening. Mel exhaled sharply, setting her notepad down.

"You can act like you don't care, but I know you do," Mel said. "I know you're smart. I know you're better than this."

Aisha finally looked up, unimpressed.

"You don't know anything about me."

Mel leaned forward. "I know what happens when girls start thinking they've got it all under control. When they start thinking the people around them care. They don't, Aisha. Not like you think they do."

For a split second, something flickered in Aisha's expression. Doubt. But it was gone just as fast.

Mel watched her stand up and walk out of the meeting room without another word.

She wanted to scream.

She had one job—to protect these kids. And Aisha was slipping away right in front of her.

She knew she was coming across as patronising, but what else could she do? She had worked so hard to get into this role, to be the kind of social worker that actually made a difference. But what if she was just like all the others? What if she was already too late?

Aisha had looked up to Kellie. At first. She had been the one to introduce her to this world, the one who made her feel like she belonged.

But something had shifted.

Kellie had started treating her differently—moodier, more passive-aggressive. Aisha noticed the way she snapped at her more often and how she suddenly stopped inviting her places unless YS asked for her.

One night, they were walking home when Kellie finally snapped.

"You think YS rates you like that?" Kellie scoffed.

"You're just a little runner, babes. Nothing special."

Aisha flinched but kept her face neutral.

"It's just a job, Kellie."

Kellie folded her arms.

"Nah. You're getting gassed. Acting like you're some big deal. Newsflash, you're not."

Aisha forced a laugh.

"Why you moving like this?"

Kellie smirked, but it didn't reach her eyes.

"Just don't get comfortable, yeah?"

Aisha felt something sharp twist in her gut. Was Kellie warning her? Or threatening her?

Kellie felt pushed aside.

YS used to trust her with everything. Now? It was all about Aisha.

She wasn't stupid. She knew exactly how this worked. The moment someone new and fresh came in, the old ones got pushed out. She refused to be one of them.

She had brought Aisha in. She had made her.

And if Aisha thought she could just slide in and take her place?

She was wrong.

But the truth was, it wasn't just about YS. It was about control. Aisha had been hers—her responsibility, her little project. And now? Now she was slipping away.

Kellie wasn't about to let that happen.

YS was watching everything.

The tension between Kellie and Aisha? He liked it. It worked in his favour. Aisha needed to see Kellie for what she was—competition.

He smirked to himself. Aisha was answering his messages the moment they came through. She was showing up when he called.

And most importantly? She was looking for his approval.

That was the key.

She was exactly where he wanted her to be.

Chapter 7: The Test

Aisha had started to feel it creep in—the shift. The way things were beginning to change. The way YS was watching her more closely, the way Kellie's hold on her felt tighter, more possessive. She didn't know when exactly it had happened, but it was there, simmering just beneath the surface.

And then one night, YS decided it was time.

They were at one of the flats, music playing low in the background, the usual crowd around—Kellie, a couple of the older boys, Shante, a few others she barely knew. Aisha had settled in, sipping on a bottle of Fanta, pretending not to notice the way YS kept glancing her way. She wasn't stupid. She knew something was coming.

And she was right.

"Ai."

She turned her head at the sound of her name. YS was sitting back on the sofa, his arm slung lazily over the backrest, his expression unreadable. But his eyes? They were locked on her.

"Come here," he said smoothly.

Aisha hesitated. Just for a second. But that second was enough to make Kellie shift uncomfortably beside her, enough to make the air in the room grow tense.

So she went.

YS pulled her down onto the sofa next to him, his hand resting lightly on her knee.

"You good, yeah?"

Aisha nodded, but something in her stomach twisted. Why did this feel different?

YS glanced around the room, then nodded at one of the boys. The guy—one of the older ones she barely knew—leaned over, passing something to YS. Aisha's breath caught when she saw it.

A small baggie. White powder.

Her stomach twisted harder.

YS held it up between two fingers, letting the light catch on it.

"You trust me, yeah?"

Aisha's throat felt dry.

"Yeah."

YS smirked, then handed her the bag.

"Good. Hold this for me."

Silence.

Aisha stared at the tiny package in her palm, the weight of it suddenly suffocating. This was different. This wasn't just sitting in a flat. This wasn't just being part of the crew. This was something else entirely.

YS watched her, his expression calm but his eyes sharp. This was a test.

She knew it. Kellie knew it.

And that's when she realised—there was no choice here. Not really.

She glanced at Kellie, searching for something, anything, but her friend wouldn't meet her eyes. Instead, Kellie just leaned back, exhaling slowly, like she had seen this happen a hundred times before.

Like she knew exactly what came next.

Aisha swallowed hard. She could feel everyone's eyes on her now, waiting, watching.

YS tilted his head slightly.

"What's wrong?"

Aisha shook her head quickly.

"Nothing."

"Then hold it," YS said again, softer this time, but there was something dangerous beneath his words.

"Just for a little bit."

Aisha curled her fingers around the bag, feeling the plastic press against her palm. Her heart was racing, but she forced herself to breathe. She couldn't mess this up.

YS smiled then, slow and approving.

"Good girl. Drop it off to Tiny for me, he's waiting in the block"

She exhaled shakily, nodding, trying to pretend this was normal. That this was fine.

As she walked off she felt the most ice-cold grip of fear in her chest.

Because deep down, she knew the truth.

She had just taken her first step in. And there was no way back.

The attack happened fast.

Aisha had just stepped outside the block after delivering the package to Tiny. Funny name, she thought, as Tiny had to be at least 6 feet 3 and was a solid lump.

When the first blow came—a fist to the side of her head, sending her stumbling forward. Shock hit her before the pain did.

She barely had time to register the voices, the laughter, before another hit landed, this time in her stomach, knocking the wind from her lungs.

"Think you're special, yeah?"

Shante's voice, sharp and venomous.

Aisha tried to push herself up, but hands gripped her hair, yanking her back. A boot connected with her ribs. Then another. Then another.

Pain exploded through her body, sharp, all-consuming.

She gasped, trying to curl in on herself, trying to protect her head, but they were everywhere. Hands, fists, kicks, voices, taunts. She couldn't fight back. She couldn't breathe.

"YS ain't yours," one of them spat, landing a kick to her back.

Aisha's vision blurred. The taste of blood filled her mouth. This wasn't stopping.

A punch to the jaw sent her sprawling onto the pavement, the impact ringing through her skull. She was going to black out.

And then—

"Shit, YS said not to hurt her too bad."

It was a whisper, but Aisha heard it, as though someone had screamed it in her face. The pain from the realisation that YS had ordered this hurt. It hurt way more than the beating she had just received.

Chapter 8: The Consequence

Aisha lay on the pavement, her body pulsating with pain, each breath dragging like broken glass through her ribs. Blood dripped from her lip, mixing with the grime beneath her. Her fingers curled into fists against the cold concrete, but she couldn't move.

Not yet.

Because the worst part wasn't the pain. It was what she had heard.

"YS said not to hurt her too bad"

YS.

Her breath hitched, a sharp stab of betrayal slicing through the fog of her pain. He had done this.

Set her up. Or, at the very least, let it happen. She was nothing to him.

The thought made her feel sick, but the footsteps that followed made her feel worse. Slow. Hesitant. Watching.

Aisha forced her swollen eyes open, her vision blurry, and saw him.

Kyle.

Her chest tightened with something sharper than pain—rage.

Why was he here? Why him? Why now?

Kyle stood frozen, his face pale, his breath uneven. Because he had seen this before.

Déjà vu slammed into him, stealing the air from his lungs. The dim glow of streetlights, the limp body on the pavement, the blood—it was happening again.

Darnell.

Kyle's stomach lurched, the image of that night flashing behind his eyes. The smell of metal and sweat. The echo of police shouts. The look on Darnell's face when he realised the setup. When he realised Kyle had betrayed him.

He had told himself it wasn't his fault. That he never wanted Darnell dead. That he was just trying to get out.

But now, looking at Aisha? He had done this.

He had left her defenceless.

His fists clenched, guilt curling around his ribs like a vice. If Darnell had been alive, this wouldn't have happened. If Kyle had made a different choice, Aisha wouldn't be lying there, beaten and broken.

Kyle swallowed hard, his throat dry. He had to do something.

"Aisha?"

Her name left his lips uncertainly, almost like he was afraid to say it.

She stirred, wincing as she tried to lift her head. Her face was swollen, her lip split, but when her eyes met his, there was no relief. No gratitude.

Only fury.

Her body shook as she inhaled sharply, forcing words through gritted teeth. "Get away from me."

Kyle's stomach twisted. "Aisha—"

"Get. Away. From. Me." The venom in her voice cut through the cold night air, sharper than any blade.

Kyle flinched, but he didn't move. Because she was right.

She struggled to sit up, biting back a groan. Her entire body screamed in protest, but the anger inside her burned hotter than the pain.

"You don't get to stand there and act like you care," she spat, her voice shaking with rage.

"You don't get to look at me like that. Like you feel bad. Like you actually give a shit."

Kyle exhaled slowly, his heart hammering against his ribs. Because he did care. He always had.

But he had let Darnell down. And in doing that, he had let her down, too.

"I never wanted this," Kyle murmured. "I never wanted him dead."

Aisha let out a broken laugh, her hands trembling as she wiped blood from her lip.

"Oh, well, that makes it fine, then, doesn't it?" Her eyes flashed with something raw, something that made Kyle's chest ache. Pain. Loss. Fury.

"You took Darnell from me," she whispered, her voice thick with emotion.

"You left me with nothing. And now you're here? For what? To feel better about yourself?"

Kyle's throat tightened. He had nothing to say to that. Because she was right.

For years, he had told himself that he was forced into setting Darnell up. That he had no choice. But choices had consequences.

And Aisha was paying for his.

The silence stretched between them, heavy, suffocating. He should leave.

But he couldn't.

Not this time.

"I know you hate me," he said quietly.

"You should. But you can't stay here, Aisha."

She clenched her jaw, her whole body trembling. She didn't want his help.

But she couldn't move. She was too weak.

And Kyle wasn't leaving. Not again.

Aisha's breath hitched, frustration and exhaustion warring inside her. Every cell in her body screamed at her to push him away. To spit in his face. To make him feel even a fraction of what she felt.

But she was tired.

She hated him. But she hated feeling helpless more.

Her head dipped slightly, her body giving in before her mind did.

"Don't touch me," she muttered, but her voice was barely above a whisper.

Kyle crouched down beside her, moving carefully, as if afraid she might shatter beneath his hands.

He lifted her gently, his arms tightening around her as she winced. She didn't resist, but she didn't lean into him either. She was stiff, rigid, holding on to her anger like a lifeline.

Kyle held onto her tightly, feeling the weight of what he had done—not just to her, but to both of them.

This wasn't redemption.

But maybe it was a start.

Chapter 9: The Fallout

Kyle walked beside Aisha, his hands shoved deep into his pockets, his face tense. The streetlights buzzed faintly overhead, casting long shadows on the pavement. The air was thick with silence, broken only by the occasional sound of Aisha's shaky breath.

Every step she took was slow, stiff, as if her entire body protested movement. Kyle wanted to offer to carry her, but he knew better. She barely even wanted his presence. As they reached the care home, Aisha hesitated at the door. She didn't want to go in. Didn't want to face what she looked like. But she couldn't stand out here forever. With a deep breath, she pushed through, the familiar, stale air hitting her as she stepped inside. She didn't expect to see Kellie waiting.

Kellie's eyes widened the moment she saw her.

"What the fuck? Aisha, what happened to you?" Her voice was sharp, but there was something else behind it—shock, maybe even guilt.

Aisha ignored her, limping past toward the bathroom. She needed to see the damage. She braced herself against the sink, gripping the edges so tightly that her knuckles turned white. Slowly, she lifted her gaze to the mirror.

Her breath caught in her throat.

Her face was a mess—her cheek swollen, her lip split, a dark bruise already forming along her jaw. She barely recognised herself.

Kellie hovered at the doorway, watching.

"Aisha, who did this?"

Aisha didn't answer. She didn't trust her voice. Didn't trust herself not to break.

Kellie stepped inside, grabbing a cloth and running it under the tap.

"Here." Her voice was softer now, almost uncertain. She pressed the damp cloth into Aisha's hand, and for once, Aisha didn't argue. She let Kellie help her.

As Kellie dabbed at the dried blood on her face, she exhaled sharply.

"Whoever did this went too far. This—this wasn't just a warning."

Aisha flinched slightly at the contact but didn't move away. She wanted to believe Kellie cared. But she couldn't shake the thought that Kellie had known. Had she been in on it?

Her phone buzzed.

She knew who it was before even looking. YS.

Aisha ignored it.

Another buzz.

Then another.

And then, it rang.

Her hands trembled as she stared at the screen. She couldn't answer. Not yet.

She let it ring out.

Kellie's phone buzzed next. Aisha watched as she pulled it out, frowning at the message before typing something back quickly.

"What are you saying to him?" Aisha's voice was low, wary.

Kellie hesitated, then held up her phone.

"I just told him you got beat up bad. That whoever did this went too far."

Aisha studied her, trying to read her expression. Was she playing both sides? Did she regret it? Or was she just scared?

Kellie licked her lips, looking almost nervous.

"Aisha, listen… I didn't know it was gonna be like this. It was just meant to be a few slaps—to scare you. That's what he said. Just to keep you in line. But this… this was brutal."

Aisha's stomach twisted. So she had known.

She let out a bitter laugh.

"And that's meant to make me feel better? That it was only meant to be 'a few slaps'?" Her voice cracked slightly at the end, but she swallowed it down, clenching her fists.

Kellie looked down, guilt flickering across her face. Maybe she hadn't expected this. Maybe she was starting to realise what she'd done.

Meanwhile, YS was fuming.

His jaw tightened as he read Kellie's text. Badly beaten? That wasn't what he had asked for. Shante had gone too far. Way too far.

He had only told her to scare Aisha, to remind her where she stood—not to lay her out like that. Now, Aisha wasn't answering.

And that was a problem.

YS sent another text. No reply.

He called her phone. No answer.

His stomach twisted slightly, an unfamiliar feeling creeping in. He needed control over his people, over his situation. And right now? Aisha was slipping away.

His temper flared as he flicked back to Kellie's chat, his thumbs moving fast.

"You fucked up."

Kellie flinched when she saw the message. She knew she had.

She tried to warn Aisha before, hadn't she? She tried to tell her not to trust too easily, not to push too far.

But now? Now she was trapped in the mess too.

YS's next text came through. More aggressive than the last.

"Call me. NOW."

Kellie's heart pounded. YS wasn't someone you ignored. And right now? He was furious. She turned her phone over, avoiding Aisha's gaze. She was scared. And for the first time, she wondered if Aisha had been right all along. Maybe she should have never let it get this far.

Chapter 10: Kyle's Walk Home

Kyle walked away from the care home with his hood up, hands stuffed into his pockets, his mind an absolute mess. The streets were quiet, the only sounds coming from the hum of distant traffic and the occasional rustle of the wind. But inside his head? It was loud. Deafening.

Aisha's voice still echoed in his ears.

"You took Darnell from me. You left me with nothing."

He let out a slow, shaky breath, staring down at the pavement as he walked. He had known she'd never forgive him, but hearing those words, feeling that hatred pour out of her like venom—it hit him harder than he'd expected. Harder than anything had in years. Kyle had spent so long convincing himself that what happened that night wasn't his fault. That it had been the only way. But now? Now, he wasn't so sure. Darnell's face flashed in his mind, the way he had looked at Kyle the second he realised what had happened. The second he knew he'd been set up. Kyle squeezed his eyes shut, as if that would somehow block the memory out. It never worked.

And then there was Aisha. Lying on the pavement, beaten, betrayed, looking at him like he was the devil himself.

Because to her? He was.

He had taken her protector away. The only person who ever really had her back. And now? She was alone. Kyle ran a hand down his face, frustration twisting in his chest. He hadn't meant for this. None of this. But what did it matter now? Darnell was dead. Aisha hated him. And nothing could change that.

His phone buzzed in his pocket, snapping him out of his thoughts. For a moment, he considered ignoring it, but when he pulled it out, he saw the name on the screen. Maya.

Kyle hesitated before answering.

"Yeah?"

Maya's voice was low, cautious. "You alright?"

Kyle let out a humourless laugh.

"Do I sound alright?"

There was a pause.

"Saw what happened to Aisha." Another pause. "She looked bad."

Kyle exhaled sharply, running a hand over his head.

"Yeah."

"You was with her?"

"Yeah."

Another pause. Too long.

Then, Maya's voice turned more serious.

"Kyle… don't get involved in this. You can't save her."

Kyle's jaw clenched. That's what they'd said about Darnell, too.

And look how that turned out.

He ended the call without saying another word, shoving his phone back into his pocket. He wasn't in the mood for warnings. Not when he had already made his choice.

Aisha might hate him. She might never forgive him.

But he wasn't going to let her end up like Darnell. Not if he could help it.

Chapter 11: YS – Born in Fire

YS sat in the dimly lit trap house, his fingers gripping his phone so tightly that his knuckles turned white. The messages from Kellie were still on the screen. Badly beaten.

This was not what was meant to happen.

Aisha wasn't supposed to be laid out like that. She was supposed to be shaken, humbled, and made to understand where she stood. Not broken. Not unreachable.

She was meant to run to him for protection. Not ignore him!

His jaw clenched as he flicked open his contacts, scrolling down to one name. Shante.

He hesitated, his thumb hovering over the call button. His blood was boiling, but beneath that? Something colder. A flicker of unease.

Aisha wasn't answering. And that was a problem.

He leaned back, exhaling slowly through his nose, trying to push away the rising anger. He was losing control, and he hated that feeling more than anything.

Six Years Ago

YS was twelve when his whole world shifted. Before that, he was just a kid—still running around with a ball, still getting told off for coming home late, still able to be innocent.

Then Shots got locked up.

He could still remember the night his mum came home after the raid. She was screaming, her voice raw with rage and grief.

"Darnell did this! He's the reason my boy's gone!"

Her words didn't even make sense to YS at first. He had known his brother was in deep, but this? This was different.

Shots and Darnell had beef. That was no secret. They had gone at it a few times—nothing out of the ordinary. But then they both got arrested after a fight. NFA'd, both of them.

And a week later? Armed police had raided Shots' mum's house and his girl's house, and everything had crumbled.

Drugs. Cash. Enough to bury him.

It wasn't a coincidence. At least, that's what Shots said before they took him away.

"That snitch Darnell put me here!"

And from that moment? Everything changed. YS wasn't a kid anymore. He wasn't allowed to be. He had to step up. The older heads started looking at him differently. Expecting more from him. Shots was gone, so now YS had to carry the weight.

He learned fast. Learned that being cold kept you safe. That being ruthless made you untouchable. And that revenge? Revenge was everything.

But it wasn't until years later that he found out Darnell had a little sister.

And that's when the plan started forming. Slow. Patient. Deadly.

Now

YS's fingers tapped against the table, his mind racing.

At first, Aisha was just another girl. Another pawn. Then he found out who she was. Who her brother was. And suddenly? She became something else entirely. He was going to own her. Then destroy her. But now? Now she wasn't answering. And that meant the game was slipping. He couldn't let that happen. His jaw tightened as he finally pressed the call button. Shante had some explaining to do.

Chapter 12: The Final Fight

Six years ago, on a cold and bitter evening, the streets belonged to the shadows of men who had lost too much.

Darnell and Shots had always been rivals. It wasn't just about territory or money—it was personal. The kind of hatred that burned through generations, passed down like an inheritance neither of them asked for. The night of their last fight was different. It wasn't just fists. It was war.

Darnell had been outside a chicken shop with two of his boys when Shots rolled up with his own crew. Tension crackled in the air like a lit fuse. Everyone knew something was about to go down.

Shots stepped forward first, his jaw tight and eyes cold.

"You thought you could move weight in my ends and no one would check you?"

Darnell smirked, the arrogance in his expression making Shots' blood boil.

"Your ends? Man, you lost control time ago."

Shots' boys tensed, shifting, waiting for the signal. Darnell didn't flinch. He was used to this dance, the circling of wolves.

Shots took another step closer, voice low, venomous.

"You think this is a game? You think I don't know what you did?"

Darnell's smirk faltered for a second. Just a second.

"What the fuck you talking about?"

Shots' nostrils flared. This was it. The moment he'd been waiting for.

"You try get man set up. You still wanna act dumb?"

Darnell's expression darkened. He took a step closer, now inches from Shots' face. Neither backed down.

"You think man set you up? If I wanted you gone, you wouldn't be standing here chatting shit."

Shots let out a dry laugh.

"Nah, see, I know you, D. You ain't gonna let no beef slide. And I ain't letting this slide either."

Before Darnell could react, Shots swung first. A heavy punch landed across Darnell's jaw, sending him stumbling back. Then it erupted. Fists, kicks, bodies slamming into walls. The sound of skin meeting skin, grunts of pain, the sickening crack of knuckles against bone. Darnell fought like a man with nothing to lose. Shots fought like a man reclaiming his pride. Blood sprayed against the pavement as Darnell landed a brutal hook to Shots' ribs, sending him crashing against a bin.

But Shots was relentless. He wiped the blood from his mouth and charged again. This wasn't about winning. This was about sending a message.

Police sirens cut through the air, blue lights flashing against the buildings.

Someone had called them. Too late.

Darnell and Shots were both dragged off the streets, cuffed, and thrown into the backs of police vans. Their crews scattered, leaving them to their fate.

23 long hours later, they were both released with no further action.

A week later, armed police stormed Shots' mum's house. His girl's place. Found everything they needed to bury him. Drugs. Cash. Evidence.

And he knew—he fucking knew—who was behind it.

As they shoved him into a van, his last words to his mum were the same words he'd carried in his heart every day since:

"That pussyhole Darnell set me up."

And YS? YS never forgot.

Chapter 13: The Realisation

Aisha sat on the edge of her bed, staring at the cracked screen of her phone. The messages were still there. Unread. Unanswered.

YS had called. Again. And again. And again.

She didn't trust him. Couldn't trust him.

She had replayed the attack in her head a hundred times. The sneering faces. The way they circled her like a pack of wolves. The way one of them had let his name slip.

He told us not to go too hard.

It made her feel sick. Because no matter how much she tried to deny it, she had been played. Everything—every little moment, every conversation, every touch—had been a lie. And the worst part? She had wanted to believe him. A tear slipped down her cheek, but she wiped it away fast. She wouldn't cry for him.

Kellie shifted awkwardly in the doorway, arms crossed. She had been silent for a while, watching Aisha like she wanted to say something but didn't know how.

Aisha finally broke the silence.

"You knew, didn't you?"

Kellie inhaled sharply, but she didn't deny it. She couldn't.

"I thought it was just a warning," Kellie admitted.

"Just something to put you in your place."

Aisha let out a bitter laugh. "You think that makes it better?"

Kellie flinched. "I didn't know they'd go that far."

Aisha shook her head, feeling cold all over. It didn't matter. Whether Kellie had known how bad it would be or not—she had still let it happen.

"I warned you," Kellie whispered.

"I told you not to get too close."

Aisha looked up at her then, her expression unreadable.

"Were you jealous?"

Kellie stiffened.

"What?"

"You wanted to be the only one he rated," Aisha said flatly.

"That's why you never warned me properly. You wanted me to slip."

Kellie's jaw tightened.

"It wasn't like that."

Aisha stared at her for a long moment.

"Yeah, it was."

Kellie didn't argue this time. Because Aisha was right.

The weight of it all crashed down on her then. She had nothing. No one. Her brother was dead. Her mum was gone. Kyle was the reason Darnell wasn't here anymore. Kellie had betrayed her. And YS?

YS had set her up.

The boy she had thought cared. The boy who had pulled her in whispered reassurances and made her feel like she belonged. It was all a game to him.

Her stomach twisted. She wasn't safe.

She had never been safe.

Aisha let out a bitter laugh, her anger bubbling over. She turned sharply to Kellie.

"You make me sick."

Kellie opened her mouth to respond, but Aisha wasn't finished.

"You knew. You stood there and let it happen. You were meant to be my friend, Kellie."

Kellie swallowed hard, her face crumbling.

"Aisha, I—"

"Fuck off."

Aisha's voice was deadly quiet, filled with something sharp and broken.

"I don't ever want to hear your voice again."

Before Kellie could say another word, Aisha slammed the door in her face, locking it behind her. She needed space. She needed to breathe.

Meanwhile, across town, in the local park, Shante sat with a group of girls and boys, laughing loudly. The streetlights flickered above them as she bragged about what she and her girls had done to Aisha.

"She didn't even fight back properly."

Shante sneered, mimicking Aisha curled up on the pavement. The others laughed, but some of them shifted uncomfortably.

"She was crying like a little bitch."

Another girl chuckled, shaking her head.

Shante grinned, basking in the attention. This was what she lived for. She was top girl. She had the ratings. She had the respect. And now everyone knew that Aisha wasn't shit.

Then her phone buzzed.

She pulled it out, still smirking—until she saw the name on the screen.

YS.

Her stomach twisted. Her fingers trembled slightly as she opened the message.

"I think me n you need to have a little chat, Shante. Don't you?"

Shante's breath caught in her throat. The air around her felt suddenly suffocating. Fear slithered down her spine.

She knew she had gone too far. She had lost control.

The truth was, she had been jealous of Aisha. Jealous of the way YS had looked at her. Jealous of the way he had spoken to her like she was special. Like she meant something. Shante was meant to be top girl. She was the one who had the respect. The status. The ratings.

And then Aisha came along.

And she was convinced—convinced—that Aisha was trying to take her place. Trying to seduce YS. That's why she had laid into her so badly. The red mist had taken over. The fear of losing YS, of being replaced, had fuelled every single kick. Every single punch.

And now?

Now YS wanted to talk.

Shante swallowed hard, the confidence draining from her body.

Because she knew.

She had fucked up.

Chapter 14: The Reckoning

YS sat alone in the darkened trap house, the air thick with the stench of stale smoke and paranoia. His fingers tapped rhythmically against his thigh as he stared at his phone screen, his message to Shante still glowing in the dim light. She had seen it. But she hadn't replied.

His jaw tightened.

YS was not a man you ignored. Especially not when you'd fucked up. He exhaled slowly, forcing himself to stay calm. Control. That was what mattered. Losing his temper was weakness, and YS refused to be weak. But this situation was slipping. Shante had let her emotions take over. That was reckless. Unacceptable. His fingers curled into fists as he replayed the photo that Kellie had sent him in his mind. Aisha. Bruised. Broken. And now, Silent.

She wasn't supposed to be silent.

He clicked his fingers absentmindedly, his mind whirring. Shante had always been useful. Always willing to do the dirty work, always eager to impress. But tonight, she had made herself a liability. And liabilities had to be dealt with.

His phone buzzed. A short, hesitant message from Shante.

"Where you at?"

YS smirked coldly. Now she was ready to talk.

Shante arrived at the block ten minutes later, her heart hammering against her ribs. The high she had felt earlier—the rush of beating Aisha down, the thrill of her crew hyping her up—had completely vanished. Now, all that was left was fear.

YS wasn't like the others. He didn't lose control. He didn't act on impulse. When YS punished someone, it was calculated. Precise. Deadly.

She stepped into the dimly lit stairwell, her hands clammy as she reached for the door to the flat. It creaked open slowly, and YS was already sitting there, watching her. Waiting. Shante swallowed hard, her mind racing. She had seen this look before. The stillness before a storm. YS felt the tension in the air; the way her breathing was slightly uneven. Good. She should be afraid. He didn't move as she stepped inside, didn't speak. Just let the silence stretch. It was almost funny. How quickly they crumbled when he stopped playing nice.

Finally, he leaned forward, elbows on his knees.

"You wanna tell me why you ignored my orders?"

Shante licked her lips, her voice coming out hoarse.

"I—I didn't ignore them. I just… I got caught up."

YS tilted his head, studying her like she was something small, something beneath him.

"Caught up?"

Shante nodded quickly, desperate to justify herself.

"I just thought she needed to be put in her place. She was moving mad, YS. Acting like she was special. Like you rated her."

YS's eyes flashed. There it was.

"Like I rated her," he repeated slowly, tasting the words.

Shante swallowed.

"Yeah, I mean—"

YS stood suddenly, the motion smooth, effortless. Controlled. Shante tensed, and YS saw it. The way her shoulders tightened, the way her breath quickened. She was scared.

"You made a mess," he murmured, eyes locked onto hers.

"And now, I have to clean it up."

Shante's stomach twisted. She had seen what YS did to people who crossed him. She didn't want to be one of them.

"I—I can fix it—"

YS cut her off with a soft chuckle. But there was no humour in it.

"Nah, you can't," he said, voice almost gentle.

"See, Shante, I let you run around thinking you were top girl, yeah? I let you feel like you were important." He leaned in slightly, his voice dropping to a whisper.

"But you forgot one thing."

Shante's pulse pounded in her ears.

"W-what?"

YS smiled, a cruel, slow stretch of his lips.

"I own you."

The words hit like a slap. Shante opened her mouth to protest, but YS held up a finger.

"You see, the thing about people like you," he continued,

"Is that you get too comfortable. You think 'cause I let you eat, 'cause I let you stand beside me, that you're untouchable."

YS shook his head slowly, clicking his tongue.

"You ain't untouchable, Shante. You're disposable."

Shante felt her breath hitch. He wasn't warning her. He was reminding her.

"YS, please—"

Before she could finish her sentence, YS's hand shot out, gripping her throat. Not hard enough to choke her. Just enough to remind her who was in control.

Shante's eyes widened in panic. She tried to pull away, but YS tightened his grip just slightly. Enough to make her freeze.

"You fucked up," he whispered.

"And I don't let people fuck up twice."

Tears pricked at the corners of Shante's eyes.

"I—I'll fix it. I swear."

YS studied her for a long moment, then finally let go. Shante stumbled back, gasping for air, her entire body shaking. She had never been scared of him before. But now? Now she knew exactly what he was.

YS stepped back, nodding to the door.

"Get the fuck out."

Shante didn't hesitate. She scrambled towards the door, flinging it open and practically running down the stairs.

As soon as she was outside, she collapsed onto a bench, her heart slamming against her chest. She had never been so close to death in her life.

And she knew one thing for sure—

YS wasn't finished with her yet.

Chapter 15: The Trap Tightens

Aisha barely ate. Barely slept. The weight of it all sat heavy in her chest, pressing down with each passing second. The call had confirmed what she already knew—she wasn't free.

She was never free.

But fear wouldn't break her. Not this time.

She shoved her phone deep into her pocket and forced herself to breathe. She had to think. She had to act.

Then the unexpected happened.

Her phone buzzed again. This time, it was a number she recognised.

YS.

Aisha's pulse hammered against her ribs as she stared at the screen. She had spent the last few days convinced that his silence meant something sinister, something final. But now? Now he was reaching out. And she had no idea what that meant.

Her hand trembled as she picked up the phone. What if she ignored it? Would that make things worse?

She hesitated. Then, before she could talk herself out of it, she answered.

"What do you want?"

His voice was soft. Too soft.

"You really think I'd let you go like that?"

Aisha's throat tightened.

"I don't belong to you."

A low chuckle.

"Nah, see, that's where you're wrong, babe."

Aisha flinched. Babe. The way he said it, the way his voice dripped with something almost affectionate—it made her skin crawl.

"I've been thinking," he continued, his tone smooth, controlled.

"Maybe I was too hard on you."

Aisha didn't respond. She didn't trust this.

YS sighed.

"You needed time. I get it. You were scared. I shouldn't have let things get out of hand like that. Shante was in my ear saying you had no manners and was always tryna sneak diss her. I told her to give you a slap if it made her feel better. No way did I ok for her to weigh you in like she did. I'm gna pattern her. Don't you worry."

Her blood ran cold. This was different. This wasn't what she expected.

He wasn't threatening her. He was reeling her back in.

"I miss you," YS murmured.

"You know that, right?"

Aisha's jaw clenched. Lies. All of it. But she didn't realise that for YS, this wasn't just a game of power anymore.

Chapter 16: Nowhere to Run

YS sat back, his fingers tapping lightly against his phone. The moment Aisha answered, he knew he had her where he wanted her. But this time, he wasn't going to use fear.

Fear made people run. Love made them stay.

It frustrated him that he had to do this. Fear had always been his sharpest weapon. His easiest tool. He liked control. He liked knowing people were too afraid to cross him. But Aisha? She was different.

She had fought back in ways he didn't expect. She had survived the beating. Survived the silence. And now she was slipping from his grip.

He couldn't let that happen.

So he softened his tone and injected warmth into his words. Let her think he cared.

"I miss you."

He could almost hear her hesitation through the phone. She wanted to believe it. She needed to believe it. YS smirked, his grip on his phone tightening. She wasn't even aware of the noose tightening around her throat. Love was a far crueler way to break someone. And when he was done with Aisha, she'd wish she had never doubted him.

Chapter 17: The Mind Games Begin

"I miss you."

"Why now?" Her voice was small, uncertain.

"Why are you calling me now?"

YS exhaled, making sure his voice sounded controlled, regretful.

"Because I needed time, Aisha. Time to see how much I fucked up. I let you down. I should have protected you."

She closed her eyes. The words were exactly what she needed to hear. Exactly what she had wished he would say. But was it real?

"I don't trust you," she whispered, barely audible.

YS ran a hand over his face, forcing a sigh of frustration but not anger.

"I get that. I deserve that. But tell me, Aisha... If you didn't trust me at all, why did you pick up?"

Her stomach dropped. He was right.

She shouldn't have answered. She shouldn't still be on the phone. But she was. She had cracked the door open just enough, and YS had slipped in before she could slam it shut.

YS leaned forward, his voice dropping to a near whisper.

"I can't change what's happened, but I swear to you, I never wanted this. You meant something to me."

Aisha swallowed hard.

"Meant?"

YS smiled at the hesitation in her voice. There it was. The first thread unraveling.

"Mean," he corrected smoothly.

"You still mean something to me."

Aisha's heart pounded. She was fighting herself. Fighting him. But she was losing.

YS sensed her internal struggle, so he gave her something softer. Something to tip her over the edge.

"You were the only real one, Aisha. The only one who saw me, not the name, not the rep. Just me."

Her breath caught in her throat. She had thought that once. Had let herself believe she was special to him. That despite the life he lived, despite everything, he cared.

Maybe he really did. Maybe she had misunderstood everything.

"I don't know, YS…" she whispered, her voice cracking.

YS smiled to himself. She was right where he wanted her.

"Then let me prove it to you," he murmured.

"Come see me."

Aisha hesitated, every logical part of her screaming no, no, no. But logic didn't matter. Not here. Not now.

Because YS had planted a seed of doubt, and doubt was all he needed.

"You know me," he continued, voice soft but steady.

"You know I don't let people in easy. I don't trust easy. But I trusted you."

Aisha felt her throat tighten. He sounded so real.

"I need you, Aisha," he murmured, his voice laced with something dangerous, something intoxicating.

"I never wanted you to get caught up in this. But you're the only one who really gets me."

Her chest ached, torn between the truth she knew and the truth she wanted. YS had always been a liar, a manipulator. But what if, this time, he wasn't?

"Okay," she whispered.

YS leaned back, triumphant. Game over. She was his again.

But in the quiet of his own mind, he felt something shift. This wasn't just about control anymore. It was something else. It was payback.

She was breaking, and he liked it.

Chapter 18: The Reunion

Aisha stood outside the block, her fingers curled tightly around her hoodie sleeves. The estate felt smaller than she remembered, like the walls had closed in overnight. A place she used to move freely now felt suffocating. And she hadn't even stepped inside yet.

Her heart pounded against her ribs, a rapid, uneven rhythm that she couldn't control. She told herself it was adrenaline. Not excitement. Not longing. Just fear.

Then why wasn't she running?

The moment she saw him standing outside the trap house, leaning against the railing with his phone in hand, something inside her twisted. He looked different.

Not in the way he dressed—tracksuit, fresh trainers, the same expensive chain around his neck. Not in the way he stood—still carrying that effortless authority, like he owned everything around him. But in his face.

There was something softer about his expression, something that made her breath catch.

And that was the most dangerous part. Because she wanted to believe in him.

YS looked up, spotting her instantly. A slow, deliberate smile spread across his face, but it wasn't the usual smirk she had come to expect. This wasn't smug or victorious. It was something else. Something deeper.

"Ai," he murmured, stepping towards her.

"You came."

The warmth in his voice threw her off balance. She expected him to be cocky, expected him to make some slick comments. But he didn't.

Aisha swallowed, forcing herself to keep her guard up.

"I don't know why I did."

YS tilted his head, studying her like she was a puzzle he was piecing back together.

"Yeah, you do."

She looked away. He was getting into her head already. **She hated that he was right.**

YS took another step closer, careful, and measured.

"I meant what I said on the phone." His voice was low, quiet, like he was afraid to push too hard.

"I fucked up. And I hate that I hurt you."

Aisha tensed. This was dangerous. This was a trap.

But his voice…

His voice was so real.

And her body betrayed her. The anger that had burned inside her for weeks flickered, just slightly, just enough for doubt to creep in. What if he really did regret it?

She didn't know what to say, so she said nothing. Her hands curled into fists at her sides, her nails digging into her skin as she tried to hold onto what little resistance she had left.

YS let the silence stretch before speaking again.

"Come inside. Just to talk."

Aisha hesitated. She needed to say no. She needed to walk away.

But he was watching her with that quiet intensity, the same way he had the first time they met, the way that made her feel like she was the only person in the world that mattered.

He nodded slowly, as if sensing her hesitation.

"You ain't gotta do nothing. Just talk."

Her heart slammed against her ribs. She had come all this way. What was the point in turning back now?

She gave him the smallest of nods.

YS smiled again, stepping aside to let her in first.

"Good girl."

The words sent a shiver down her spine. Not because she hated them. But because she didn't.

And that scared her more than anything.

Because YS wasn't just trying to win her back. He was making her forget why she ever left.

Chapter 19: The Weight of Guilt

Kyle sat alone in his flat, the only light coming from the dim glow of his phone screen. His stomach twisted as he scrolled through the messages Aisha had ignored. She had gone back to him. He should've seen this coming. He should've known YS would pull her back in, just like the streets pulled him back every time he swore he was out. But knowing didn't make it hurt any less. He rubbed his face with his hands, frustration knotting in his chest. What the fuck was he supposed to do? He had already failed Darnell. He had been the one to set him up, thinking he was doing the right thing, thinking it would save him. Instead, it got him killed. And now Aisha was next.

The thought made his chest tighten. He couldn't let it happen. He wouldn't.

But what could he say that she would believe? He was part of the reason she had no one. Part of the reason she had nowhere to run. Why would she trust him? He clenched his jaw, memories of the past crashing over him like a tidal wave. The warehouse. The gunshots. The blood. Darnell's body hitting the ground. His hands trembled. He had told himself that setting Darnell up was necessary. That it had been his only way out. That the system was going to do it anyway—he just sped up the process. But when he looked in the mirror, he didn't see a survivor. He saw a traitor. A rat. A snake. And now, Aisha was walking straight into the same fate.

He exhaled shakily, gripping his phone tighter. He had to stop this. Even if it meant facing his past. Even if it meant putting himself in the firing line.

Because if he let YS take her, if he let Aisha end up like Darnell...

Then he'd never be able to live with himself.

Chapter 20: The Web Tightens

Three months had passed, and Aisha was deeper in YS's world than she had ever been. He owned her now. Not in chains, not in bruises, but in something worse. Something she couldn't break free from.

It started slow. Little things. Sleeping in his bed, feeling his warmth, the way his arm would tighten around her waist as if to remind her that she was his. The first time they slept together, he had whispered things into her ears—things she had never heard before—words that should have made her feel special and wanted.

Instead, they made her feel trapped.

But when morning came, his voice turned cautious.

"Keep this between us, yeah?"

She had frowned, still hazy with sleep.

"Why?"

YS kissed her forehead, fingers running through her hair.

"Kellie, Shante… They move mad when they get jealous. Ain't tryna deal with all that right now."

Aisha had nodded, telling herself it didn't matter. But deep down, something about it felt off. She told herself that as long as he still held her at night, as long as he still whispered her name, she was different. She was special. But she wasn't stupid. Something had shifted.

On the surface, things were fine. YS treated her well—better than she'd seen him treat anyone. He made sure she was always taken care of, always had money in her pocket, and always had a place beside him. But Aisha knew better.

There were cracks in the illusion.

She felt it when YS would get phone calls and step outside, when conversations stopped the moment she walked into the room. She felt it in the way Kellie's eyes lingered on her, the resentment barely hidden beneath fake smiles. And worst of all, she felt it in herself.

She wasn't happy.

But she couldn't say that out loud. Not to him. Not to anyone. Because what was the alternative? Going back to the care home? Being alone? She wasn't sure which was worse anymore. The worst part was the way she had changed. She had stopped asking questions. The first time she had asked YS where he went late at night, his smile had been easy, but his eyes weren't.

"Don't worry about it."

The second time, his jaw had tightened.

"I said don't worry about it."

She didn't ask again.

She told herself it was love. That she was protecting what they had. But deep down, she knew the truth.

She was afraid.

That night, she lay beside him, staring at the ceiling while he slept. His arm was heavy over her waist, his breathing steady. Anyone looking in would think this was normal. That this was love. But Aisha felt like she was suffocating.

She thought about the girl she used to be. The one who laughed without checking who was watching, who had dreams bigger than these four walls. Where had she gone?

She turned her head, looking at YS in the dim light. He looked peaceful. He looked like the boy she once believed he was.

But she knew better now.

Still, she didn't move. Didn't get up. Didn't leave.

Because even though she hated herself for it… she didn't know how.

Chapter 21: YS's Game

YS wasn't asleep. He could feel the tension in Aisha's body beside him; the way her breathing had changed, slower but not relaxed. She was thinking too much. Again.

His grip on her waist tightened slightly, not enough to wake her fully, but enough to remind her he was there. That he wasn't letting go.

YS had always known control was about balance. Give them what they need, but not too much. Keep them guessing, keep them wanting. Aisha was smart. Smarter than most girls he had dealt with. But that didn't matter. Because she wanted to believe in him.

And that was enough.

He had played this perfectly. He had made her feel safe, but not secure. Wanted, but never truly claimed. Because once a girl thought she had you, she stopped trying. And YS didn't need Aisha to feel safe. He needed her to need him.

She had stopped asking questions. That was good. That meant she was settling into her place, accepting what she was. But tonight, something felt off. She was too quiet. Too distant.

He didn't like that.

His eyes opened, adjusting to the darkness. He looked at her, the way she stared at the ceiling, lost in thought. She was slipping again. Thinking too much. Doubting.

YS shifted slightly, pressing a soft kiss to her shoulder.

"You good?"

Aisha flinched, just barely. But he caught it.

She forced a small smile.

"Yeah. Just tired."

Lies.

YS ran his fingers slowly down her arm, a move designed to relax, to remind.

"You know I got you, yeah?"

She nodded, but it wasn't real. He felt it. She was pulling away.

YS stared at the ceiling now too, his mind whirring. He had to fix this. Quickly.

Because if Aisha was starting to think about leaving…

He'd have to make sure she knew there was nowhere to go.

He let out a slow breath, his mind wandering back—back to when he still had dreams.

Before all this, before Shots went down, before Darnell ruined everything, YS wanted something different. Football.

He was good at it, too. Coaches told him he had potential and that he could go far. That he could be something.

But that was before his brother was taken. Before Darnell fucked everything up.

When Shots got locked up, everything changed. Suddenly, it wasn't about chasing dreams—it was about stepping up, filling his brother's shoes, and making sure their name still held weight. He didn't have a choice. The game didn't give you choices.

Now, looking at Aisha beside him, YS smirked to himself.

This was just balance.

Darnell took his brother from him. He was just taking something back.

Aisha thought this was love. Thought she meant something to him. And in a way, she did. Just not in the way she hoped.

He leaned in, his lips brushing against her ear as he whispered, "Go to sleep, babe."

Aisha exhaled softly, her body relaxing slightly.

YS smirked against her skin. Yeah. That's right. Stay right where I want you.

Because she wasn't going anywhere.

Chapter 22: The Breaking Point

No one really talked about what happened to Shante.

One day, she was top girl—loud, confident, untouchable. The next, she was a ghost. A mess. Strung out. Gone.

No one knew how it happened. Except YS.

Shante had fucked up. The attack on Aisha? She went too far.

And YS didn't tolerate mistakes. Not ones that made him look weak.

He could have just cut her off. He could have just cast her aside like he did to other girls when they stopped being useful. But Shante had been useful—and more than that, she had been loyal. So YS made an example out of her in a way that was worse than death. He made her nothing.

It started with the beating. That part was expected. No one crossed YS and walked away without feeling it. He made sure everyone in the crew saw what happened to girls who overstepped.

But that wasn't the real punishment. That came after.

She had barely been conscious when it happened. Bruised, broken, sobbing into the floor of a cold, empty flat, pleading for another chance.

YS had crouched beside her, voice smooth, almost gentle.

"You wanna make it up to me, yeah?"

Shante had nodded, desperate, eyes swollen shut from the punches, blood drying on her split lip.

YS had smiled.

"Good. Then stay still."

She hadn't understood. Not until one of his boys rolled up her sleeve. Not until the belt was tightened around her arm, the needle pressed against her skin.

She had started screaming then, begging, thrashing weakly, but she was too hurt, too broken to fight back.

YS held her down.

"Relax. It's just one time."

The needle slid in. The plunger was pushed. And just like that, she was gone.

Shante never stood a chance after that. The next hit came easy. Then the next. Before long, she wasn't Shante anymore.

She was just another nitty on the ends, wandering the streets in search of the next high, desperate, willing to do anything for it.

And the worst part? No one cared.

The same boys that used to fear her now laughed when they saw her. The same girls that used to follow her now crossed the street when she stumbled past. She was nothing now. Less than nothing.

And YS? He never mentioned her name again. She was erased.

Aisha had heard the rumours, but it wasn't until she saw Shante with her own eyes that the fear truly set in.

It was late, and she had been out running an errand for YS, still wrapped up in his world, still trying to convince herself she wasn't trapped. She had seen the figure slumped against the bus stop, wrapped in layers of dirty clothes, her once-perfect hair tangled, her face gaunt, and her empty eyes staring at nothing. It had taken Aisha a moment to recognise her.

Shante.

Her stomach twisted violently. How? How had this happened?

She had walked over, hesitated, then crouched beside her.

"Shante?"

Shante's head lolled to the side, her pupils pinpricks, and her breath was slow and uneven. She blinked sluggishly, taking a few seconds to register Aisha. When she did, she let out a dry, humourless laugh.

"Look at you," she slurred.

"Still YS's favourite."

Aisha's throat tightened.

"Shante… what happened?"

Another laugh, this one weaker.

"What do you think happened?"

Silence.

Aisha knew. She already knew. Shante studied her for a long time, her cracked lips pulling into a smirk that was more pain than amusement.

"You think you're different, yeah?"

Aisha's heart pounded.

"I don't—"

"You're not," Shante cut her off. "You're just next."

The words sent ice through Aisha's veins.

She took a shaky step back, but Shante grabbed her wrist, fingers like claws, her grip surprisingly strong.

"Run," she whispered, breath hot against Aisha's skin.

"Run before you end up like me. Or worse"

Aisha yanked away.

She turned and walked off, fast, then faster, until she was running. She didn't stop until she was back in the flat, back in YS's world, back in his arms.

Safe.

No. Not safe. Just in deeper.

And that night, as she lay awake beside him, the words played over and over in her head.

You're just next.

Chapter 23: No Way Out

Kyle couldn't shake the guilt. It clung to him like smoke, thick and suffocating. He had set up Darnell, and now Aisha was drowning in the same world that had killed her brother. He had tried to reach out, sending messages she never answered, hanging around places he thought she might be, but Aisha was avoiding him. And he didn't blame her.

But that didn't mean he was going to stop.

Kyle had spent months trying to live with the blood on his hands, convincing himself that he had no choice. But now, looking at what had become of Aisha, he knew that was bullshit. He had a choice back then, and he chose wrong.

He wouldn't make that mistake again.

YS had started watching Aisha more closely. He didn't like unanswered messages. He didn't like her looking distracted.

One night, as they sat in his flat, YS scrolling through his phone, he suddenly spoke.

"You been talking to anyone?"

Aisha tensed.

"What do you mean?"

YS didn't look up.

"You know what I mean."

Her stomach knotted.

"No."

YS finally turned to face her, his expression unreadable.

"Good. 'Cause if I find out you've been chatting to any man, it's gna get peak for you."

Aisha nodded quickly, keeping her face blank, but inside her thoughts were spiraling.

YS leaned in, his voice low and dangerous.

"I don't like disrespect, Ai. And talking to some dickhead behind my back? That's disrespect."

She swallowed hard, forcing herself to nod again. Stay calm. Stay quiet. Stay in control. YS studied her for a long moment, then smirked, pressing a kiss to her cheek.

"That's my girl."

Aisha felt sick.

Kyle didn't expect to see her that day.

He had been walking through the estate, hood up, hands shoved deep in his pockets, when he spotted her across the road. She looked different.

Tired. Smaller somehow. Like she was folding in on herself.

Before he could think twice, he crossed the road.

"Aisha."

She stopped in her tracks. She didn't look surprised—just wary. Like she had been expecting this.

Kyle kept his voice calm.

"I just wanna talk."

Aisha hesitated. She knew she shouldn't. She should keep walking; pretend she hadn't seen him. But something in his voice made her pause. He sounded like he cared. And that made her want to cry. She took a shaky breath.

"Kyle, I—"

"Oi, what the fuck is this?"

Aisha's blood ran cold. YS.

He was storming towards them, jaw tight, eyes blazing with fury. Kyle stepped back instantly, but it was too late.

YS shoved Aisha aside and squared up to Kyle.

"You got some fucking nerve coming round here."

Kyle held his hands up.

"I'm not looking for trouble. Was just seeing if Aisha was ok"

YS scoffed.

"Yeah? 'Cause last time I checked, you set up her brother to get smoked. And now you wanna be her little saviour?" He laughed, but there was no humour in it. Just rage. Just venom.

"You're a fucking snake, you know that?"

Kyle clenched his jaw but said nothing. While YS spoke to Aisha, Kyle walked away.

YS turned to Aisha.

"You chatting to him now? That what we're doing?"

Aisha shook her head frantically.

"No, I swear, I—"

YS cut her off, his voice sharp.

"Then why the fuck you out here, smiling in his face like some dickhead? You fancy him or something?"

Aisha felt the air get knocked from her lungs.

"What? No!"

YS stepped closer, his presence overwhelming.

"Prove it."

She blinked.

"What?"

YS's smile was slow and cruel.

"You wanna prove you ain't a slag? That you ain't running round with your brother's killer like some dumb bitch?"

Aisha's hands trembled.

"YS, please—"

"Arrange to meet him, then bring him to me," YS said, his voice almost casual.

"If you ain't on some snake shit, you'll do it."

Aisha's whole body went numb. He wanted her to betray the only person who had ever tried to save her. But this person had also set up her brother and got him killed.

Her eyes flicked to Kyle, who was walking away now.

This was a test.

One she couldn't fail.

And the worst part?

She already knew what she was going to do.

Chapter 24: The Setup

Aisha's hands trembled as she stared at her phone. One message. That's all it would take. One text to Kyle. One invitation.

One trap.

She typed out the message, hesitating with her thumb hovering over the send button. Her stomach twisted violently. Could she really do this? YS was watching her. Always watching. Even now, as he sat across the room scrolling through his phone, she knew he was waiting.

Waiting for her to prove her loyalty.

She had no choice.

Her fingers moved on autopilot.

Aisha: You about? Need to talk. Just me.

Kyle responded almost instantly.

Kyle: You okay?

She hesitated. Then typed:

Aisha: Just meet me. Same place. Half an hour.

She pressed send.

She felt like she was going to be sick.

YS smirked when he saw her put her phone down.

"That's my girl."

Aisha forced a nod, her face blank. She was good at this now. Good at pretending. Good at lying to herself.

Inside she was screaming.

She didn't want to do this. But if she didn't… she already knew what YS was capable of. She had seen what happened to Shante. She had felt what happened to girls who crossed him. And he had already planted the seed of doubt. Would he believe she was setting Kyle up if she didn't go through with it? Or would she be next?

YS stood up, cracking his knuckles.

"You bring him. We'll do the rest."

Aisha swallowed hard. She nodded again. She was in too deep.

Kyle was waiting for her at the park, hands in his pockets, shoulders tense. He looked nervous.

Good. He should be.

But Aisha couldn't stop the guilt from spreading through her chest like poison. He had always tried to protect her, and now she was leading him into danger. Her heart hammered as she approached. Every fibre of her being screamed at her to stop. To tell him to run. But she couldn't. YS had eyes everywhere.

Kyle frowned.

"Aisha, what's going on?"

She forced herself to meet his eyes. Lie. Just lie.

"I just…" she bit her lip, forcing her voice to shake.

"I don't know what to do anymore, Kyle."

Kyle's expression softened immediately.

"Come with me, Ai. We'll figure it out."

Aisha's stomach clenched. For a split second, she almost did it. Almost reached for his hand. She almost let herself believe she could just walk away.

Then she saw movement in the distance. YS's boys. Waiting. Watching.

Her pulse skyrocketed. There was no way out.

She took an unsteady breath.

"Just walk with me. Please."

Kyle hesitated, then nodded.

As they walked, Aisha could feel the seconds slipping away. She was running out of time.

Kyle's voice was low, cautious.

"You know I'd do anything for you, right?"

Aisha nearly tripped over her own feet. The words hit harder than any punch. He still cared.

She forced herself to keep moving.

"Yeah," she whispered. "I know."

Kyle sighed.

"Then talk to me, Ai. I know you don't want this."

Her breath hitched. He was right. But what does it matter now? What could she do? If she warned him, YS would know. If she ran, YS would find her. She turned her head slightly, just enough to see YS's boys moving closer behind them.

Kyle followed her gaze. His shoulders tensed. He knew something was wrong now.

Aisha's throat tightened. She was about to destroy him.

Unless…

No. No, no, no. Don't think like that. There was no unless.

She had made her choice.

Kyle gave her a look then—one she'd never forget. A look of realisation. A look of betrayal.

And it was in that moment Aisha realised something too. This choice? It wasn't hers at all. It never had been.

Chapter 25: The Choice

Kyle knew.

Aisha could see it in his face, in the way his eyes darted to the shadows behind them, in the way his breath hitched slightly. He wasn't stupid.

Neither was she.

She had walked him straight into a trap, and he had let her. Maybe some part of him had wanted to believe she wouldn't do it. Maybe some part of him still believed she wouldn't.

Aisha's heart pounded. This was it.

She could still warn him. Right now. She could whisper a single word, a single movement that told him to run.

But then what? YS would know. He would find her. And this time, she wouldn't get another chance.

Kyle's jaw clenched as YS's boys stepped out of the shadows, surrounding them. His gaze flickered back to Aisha. He wasn't looking at her with anger. He was looking at her with heartbreak.

"Aisha."

It was barely a whisper, but she flinched like he had screamed it.

YS approached then, slow, deliberate, a smirk playing on his lips. He had been waiting for this moment. The moment Aisha would prove, once and for all, that she belonged to him. That there was no going back.

"Good girl," he murmured, brushing his fingers against Aisha's arm. Ownership. That's what this was. And she knew it.

Kyle's expression darkened.

"She's not your girl."

YS let out a short laugh.

"You sure? 'Cause from where I'm standing, it looks like she made her choice."

Aisha squeezed her eyes shut. This wasn't her choice. It never had been.

YS studied Kyle, his smirk fading slightly. He hated him. Kyle was a loose end, a reminder of a past YS wanted erased. And worst of all, YS saw the way Aisha looked at him—the way her face softened, the way she hesitated. It disgusted him. Despite it being this little prick that set her brother up to be to killed by feds. One of YS's boys shoved Kyle hard, sending him stumbling back. Aisha opened her mouth—to do what, she didn't even know. But Kyle recovered quickly, standing tall. He wouldn't beg. He wouldn't run.

YS tilted his head, amused. Kyle's bravery was pathetic. Admirable, maybe. But still pathetic.

"You really thought you could just waltz back in and save her? That's not how this works, bruv."

He glanced at Aisha.

"Tell him."

Aisha's breath caught in her throat. She stared at Kyle, at the boy who had tried to protect her, who had once been the only person to truly see her. And now she was the reason he was about to get hurt. YS's fingers flexed at his sides. He could feel Aisha's hesitation like a pulse in the air. She wasn't moving fast enough. She wasn't proving herself.

His voice dropped, all amusement gone.

"Tell him, Aisha."

She swallowed hard. Say it. Say anything. Say what he needs to hear to stay alive.

But before she could, Kyle exhaled, shaking his head.

"I get it now," he muttered.

"You're too scared."

YS clicked his tongue. Wrong answer.

"Shame, really. I was kinda hoping you'd put up more of a fight."

Kyle barely had time to react before the first punch landed. YS watched, his expression unreadable. He felt nothing as his boys descended, as the sound of fists meeting flesh echoed through the night. This wasn't about Kyle. This was about Aisha. About reminding her.

She had nowhere else to go.

Aisha let out a strangled sound, stepping forward on instinct, but YS grabbed her wrist, holding her back. His grip was firm, bruising.

"Nah, you wanted this, yeah? Watch."

She hadn't wanted this. She had never wanted this.

But still, she stood there. And watched.

Watched as Kyle fought back, as fists connected, as blood sprayed onto the pavement. Watched as the boy who had once saved her was destroyed because of her. But he was also the person who got Darnell killed. Her inner conflict was torturing her. And when it was over, when Kyle lay crumpled on the ground, barely conscious, YS finally let her go. Aisha fell to her knees beside him, hands trembling as she hovered over his broken form. His breaths were ragged, his face barely recognisable beneath the bruises. Kyle's swollen eyes fluttered open, just barely. His lips cracked into the faintest of smiles. And then he whispered the words that shattered her completely.

"I forgive you."

YS scoffed, rolling his eyes. Pathetic.

Aisha choked on a sob.

She had lost.

Kyle had lost.

And YS had won.

Again.

Chapter 27: The Spiral

Kyle woke up to the steady beeping of a heart monitor and the sterile smell of disinfectant burning his nose. His body ached in ways he had never felt before—a deep, throbbing pain that seemed to settle in his bones. For a moment, everything was a blur. The white ceiling, the IV drip taped to his arm, the rhythmic hum of the machines. But then the memories crashed into him all at once.

Fists. Boots. Blood. YS's smile. Aisha's face—fearful, broken.

His breath hitched. Aisha.

"Hey, hey—easy."

A soft voice pulled him from his thoughts. He turned his head slowly, wincing at the sharp pain that shot through his ribs. Maya sat beside him, worry etched into every feature. Kyle swallowed, his throat raw.

"Maya?"

She exhaled in relief.

"You're awake."

He tried to sit up, but pain seared through his body, forcing him back down. Maya reached out, pressing a hand to his arm.

"Don't. You need to rest."

Kyle clenched his jaw, eyes flickering around the room.

"What… what happened?"

Maya's brows furrowed.

"You tell me. You were found on the estate, barely breathing. Who did this to you?"

Kyle hesitated. He saw the concern in her eyes, in the way she leaned forward, waiting for him to name names. But he wouldn't. Because despite everything, despite what they thought, he wasn't a snitch.

He let out a slow breath.

"I… I don't remember."

Maya's eyes narrowed.

"Kyle."

He turned his head away, staring at the ceiling.

"I said I don't remember."

Silence hung between them. Maya sighed, shaking her head, but she didn't push.

Kyle closed his eyes, but the images wouldn't leave him. YS standing over him, smiling like he had already won. The way Aisha had flinched when YS touched her. The way she looked at him before it all went black.

I forgive you.

The words echoed in his mind, but now they felt hollow.

Because Kyle finally understood something.

He couldn't be the one to save her.

And that truth hurt more than the broken bones ever could.

Chapter 28: Six Months Later

Six months had passed, but to Aisha, it felt like a lifetime. She barely recognised herself anymore. The girl she used to be—the one who dreamed, who laughed, who had hope—was gone. What remained was someone else entirely. Someone YS had created.

Her days blurred together—early morning drops, late-night pickups, silent car journeys, cold hotel rooms. She didn't ask questions anymore. She just did what she was told.

YS had made sure of that.

Her body moved on autopilot, but her mind? That was different. The cracks were starting to show. She would catch herself staring at her reflection in bathroom mirrors, trying to find something familiar. But all she saw was a stranger. Tired eyes. Hollow cheeks. A girl running on empty. She had stopped checking her phone months ago. Stopped wondering if Kyle would ever reach out again. He wouldn't. He had given up on her. And maybe he was right to. YS still had her under his grip, but something had shifted. She wasn't scared anymore. Not in the way she used to be.

Now? She was numb.

And that terrified her more than anything.

Aisha's weed addiction had spiralled. What started as a way to escape reality had turned into a way to function. She smoked all the time now, dulling the fear, the anger, and the whispers in her head telling her she had lost herself.

But the more she smoked, the more paranoid she became.

And she was angry. Angry at everything. Angry at YS for turning her into this. Angry at herself for letting it happen. But most of all, angry at the other girls—the ones who still played their parts like nothing was wrong.

Especially Kellie.

That fake, jealous, backstabbing bitch. Aisha saw the way Kellie looked at her, the way she still tried to stay in YS's good books. Like she was waiting for Aisha to fall so she could take her place. Like she wanted Aisha gone. One night, as they sat in the flat, Kellie made some offhand remark. Something sharp, something designed to cut.

"Damn, Ai. You look rough. YS really got you running ragged, huh?"

Aisha froze mid-smoke, her blood turning to fire. Kellie was laughing under her breath, but Aisha wasn't stupid.

The room went silent.

Then, without thinking, Aisha snapped.

She lunged, the blunt falling from her fingers as she swung. The first punch sent Kellie crashing back. The second split her lip. Aisha didn't stop. Months of anger, paranoia, resentment—all of it exploded out of her. She barely registered the screaming, the hands trying to pull her back. She was gone. Kellie was curled up on the floor, shielding herself, but Aisha was relentless.

She spat on her.

A slow, deliberate act of pure hatred.

The room stilled.

Even YS looked taken aback.

For the first time in a long time, Aisha saw something flicker in his expression—not anger, not amusement. Something closer to calculation. She had changed. And he knew it. YS watched the scene unfold, leaning back slightly. He had always known Aisha had fire in her. But this? This was different. Kellie whimpered on the floor, blood dripping from her mouth, eyes wide with terror. YS's lips curled slightly as he exhaled. There was no remorse in Aisha. No hesitation. He had pushed her and broken her down piece by piece. And now she had snapped.

Aisha's chest heaved, her fists still clenched. She didn't even seem to notice the tension in the room or the way the others were watching her. Like she was something dangerous.

YS let the silence stretch before he finally spoke, his voice low.

"Damn, Ai." He chuckled, shaking his head.

Aisha wiped the back of her hand across her mouth, eyes dark and empty. She didn't answer. Something inside her had finally snapped. She wasn't scared anymore. She wasn't even numb.

Now? She just didn't give a fuck.

YS smirked.

Chapter 29: Breaking Free?

Aisha had changed, and everyone knew it.

She could feel it in the way the others moved around her now—cautious, like she was unpredictable, a ticking time bomb no one wanted to set off. Even YS seemed to be watching her differently, a flicker of something new in his eyes when he looked at her. Was it amusement? Curiosity? Or was it suspicion?

She didn't care.

She had stopped caring about a lot of things.

Her outburst against Kellie had been a turning point. She should have felt something about it—guilt, regret, even pride—but there was just... nothing. She spent her nights high, her mind floating somewhere between reality and oblivion. Weed was her only escape, but even that was starting to turn against her. The paranoia crept in more frequently, the whispers in her mind telling her that she was losing control, that YS was watching too closely, that she was teetering on the edge of something dangerous.

And then came the moment she knew things were shifting.

YS had given her a job—a simple drop, nothing she hadn't done a hundred times before. But this time, she didn't go.

She sat on a park bench instead, staring at her phone, gripping it so tightly her knuckles turned white.

She could just leave. Right now. Walk away. Disappear.

But she didn't move.

She felt him before she saw him. YS had that presence—one that turned the air thick, made everything around him colder.

"You're slipping, Ai."

She exhaled slowly before turning her head. He was standing over her, hands in his pockets, his expression unreadable.

She met his gaze, forcing herself not to look away.

"So?"

YS let out a low chuckle, shaking his head.

"So... I don't like that."

Aisha's heart pounded, but she forced herself to stay still and act like she didn't care.

"Then don't watch me."

For a moment, YS just stared at her. Then, quicker than she could react, he grabbed her wrist, yanking her up so she was forced to face him properly. His grip was like iron, pressing down on her bones.

"You think you're untouchable now?" His voice was quiet, but there was danger in it.

"'Cause you battered Kellie? 'Cause you move like you don't give a fuck?" He tilted his head, his smile sharp.

"That's cute."

Aisha gritted her teeth, her pulse hammering in her ears. She wasn't scared of him. Not anymore.

But she wasn't stupid either.

She kept her voice steady.

"Let go of me."

YS didn't move, his grip tightening slightly.

"See, I thought breaking you would keep you in line," he murmured, his eyes flickering with something dark.

"But maybe I was wrong. Maybe you need reminding who runs this shit."

Aisha didn't flinch, but inside, something twisted violently.

This was it. The moment she had been avoiding.

She had pushed too far. And now, YS was about to remind her exactly who she belonged to.

YS watched her, waiting, calculating. He wasn't just going to punish her—he was going to make an example of her.

Unless she did something first.

Her breath steadied, her mind racing. If she was going to get out, it had to be now.

Chapter 30: No More Chains

Aisha had never known real fear until this moment. Not the kind that makes your heart race for a few seconds, but the kind that settles deep in your bones, sinking its claws into your skin. The kind that tells you this is it.

Run, Aisha. Now.

YS's grip tightened around her wrist, his fingers digging into her skin. She could feel the pressure and the silent message he was sending her. You don't get to walk away.

But this time? She wasn't going to let him win.

Aisha's breathing slowed. Her mind raced through the possibilities. Fight or run? Either way, she had to move now.

YS smirked, tilting his head as if reading her thoughts.

"You really think you got a choice, Ai?" His voice was low, threatening. Daring her to do something.

She twisted her arm sharply, breaking free from his grip just enough to shove him backward with everything she had. It caught him off guard, and in that split second, Aisha ran. YS staggered, but as soon as he regained his balance, his expression darkened. She actually ran.

A slow smile curled across his lips.

"You think you're free?" he muttered under his breath, already pulling out his phone.

"Nah, Ai. You just made it fun."

He wasn't angry. He was excited. The chase was always the best part.

YS barked orders into his phone, sending his boys after her. She wouldn't get far.

Aisha's lungs burned as she sprinted through the estate, weaving through alleyways, past familiar corners that had once been safe but now felt like death traps. She had no plan. Nowhere to go. But she knew one thing—she wasn't going back.

Her phone buzzed violently in her pocket, but she ignored it. YS. His boys. She could already hear them moving, the shouts in the distance as they realised what she'd done. They were coming for her.

Aisha's legs screamed in protest, but she kept going. She had spent too long in YS's world, trapped under his control, letting him dictate every part of her life. But not anymore.

Not. Anymore.

She needed to disappear. Now.

She turned down a side street, nearly crashing into a parked car as she staggered, gasping for breath. Her chest heaved. Where do I go? Who do I trust?

And then, like fate, a voice in her head whispered a name. Kyle.

Her stomach twisted. Kyle. After everything? She had set him up. She had watched YS's boys destroy him. She had seen the hurt in his eyes, the betrayal. And yet…

He was the only person who had ever really given a fuck about her.

But could she do it? Could she go back to him now, after everything she had done? After she had been the one to lead him into that beating? Maybe I deserve this. Maybe I should just keep running until they catch me. Footsteps pounded behind her, getting closer.

Aisha gritted her teeth. Nah. Fuck that.

Kyle had every reason to hate her, but he wasn't YS. He wouldn't hurt her. He wouldn't try to break her like YS had.

She had no choice.

No more thinking. No more chains. Aisha forced her legs to move again, this time with a destination in mind. She ran straight for the one person she once swore she'd never need again.

Chapter 31: The Reckoning

Aisha's heart hammered as she banged on Kyle's door, her breath ragged, her body trembling from exhaustion and fear. Every nerve in her body was screaming at her to keep running, but she had nowhere left to go. This was it. She had thrown herself at his mercy. And she didn't even know if he'd open the door. Behind her, the street was too quiet. She knew what that meant. YS's boys were nearby. Watching. Waiting.

The door swung open, and Kyle stood there, frozen, his expression unreadable. But Aisha saw the flicker of something in his eyes—fear. She had never seen Kyle scared before. Not like this. And it made her stomach turn. Aisha's lips parted, but no words came out. How do you even begin to apologise for something like this? Kyle's eyes swept over her—disheveled, shaking, her clothes torn from where she'd scraped against a brick wall during the chase. She looked exactly like how she felt—broken.

Finally, she choked out.

"Please."

For a second, Kyle didn't move. His jaw clenched, his fists curled at his sides. Every part of him wanted to slam the door in her face.

Then, with a sharp exhale, he stepped aside.

"Get in."

She stumbled past him, her body sagging with relief, but the feeling didn't last long. As soon as the door shut, Kyle turned to her, his jaw tight. The silence between them was suffocating.

"You got some nerve," he muttered, his voice low and controlled. Too controlled.

Aisha swallowed hard.

"Kyle, I—"

"Shut up."

Her breath hitched. She had expected anger, but this… this was something else. Something colder. Kyle ran a hand over his face, exhaling harshly.

"You set me up, Aisha. You let them do that to me." His voice cracked slightly on the last word, but he recovered quickly, masking it with something harder. Something almost hateful.

Aisha flinched. She deserved that.

"I know," she whispered.

Kyle's fists clenched at his sides. He stared at her for a long moment before shaking his head.

"Why are you here?"

Aisha hesitated, then looked him straight in the eye.

"Because I don't have anywhere else to go."

Kyle let out a bitter laugh.

"That's cute, but am I supposed to care?"

Before Aisha could respond, a loud knock rattled the door. Her stomach dropped. Kyle's body tensed. His gaze flickered to her, then to the door.

"Who the fuck is that?"

Aisha's mouth went dry. She already knew.

Another knock, harder this time.

Then, a voice.

"Come on, Ai. You know better than this."

YS.

Kyle's breath came in sharp, panicked bursts. His skin felt ice-cold, and his heart slammed against his ribs. No. Not again. Not him. The memories hit like a sledgehammer—the fists, the blood, the laughter, the feeling of powerlessness. He wanted to run. He had never wanted to run from anything in his life.

YS knocked again, his voice smooth, patient.

"Kyle, my guy. Open up. I just wna chat."

Kyle's entire body stiffened. He knew that voice. The voice that haunted his dreams. The voice of the man who had broken him. Silence stretched thick in the air. Then, YS chuckled, his tone laced with amusement. But underneath it, there was something lethal.

"You can't hide from me, Aisha."

Aisha pressed herself against the wall, her entire body trembling. She wasn't free. She was never free.

YS's voice turned colder.

"You belong to me."

Kyle's fists curled so tightly his nails dug into his palms. He wanted to fight, but he was drowning in fear.

But then he saw Aisha.

Her face was pale, her lips pressed together to stop them from shaking. She looked like him that night. And just like that, the fear turned to rage. A storm was coming.

And there was no way to stop it.

Chapter 32: Nowhere to Run

The first bang on the door made Aisha flinch so hard she felt her breath catch. YS had found them. Already. Kyle's entire body tensed beside her. She could hear his breathing—shallow, erratic. He was frozen. Another knock. Harder this time. More like a warning than a greeting.

"I'm not gonna ask again, Kyle." YS's voice was calm. Too calm.

Aisha's stomach twisted. Her skin prickled with ice. She had heard that tone before. It was the tone he used right before something bad happened. Kyle swallowed, his throat bobbing. Aisha could see it in his eyes—the terror clawing at him, the memory of the last time YS got his hands on him.

YS knocked again, slower this time. He was enjoying this.

"I ain't got all night."

Kyle didn't move. Didn't even blink. He was gripping the edge of the table, his knuckles bone-white. Aisha's pulse pounded against her ribs. This was her fault. Again. She had dragged Kyle back into this nightmare. Again. Before she could think, she grabbed his wrist, her voice barely above a whisper.

"We have to run."

Kyle turned to her, his eyes wild.

"Where?"

She had no answer.

And then—

CRACK.

The door splintered off its hinges.

YS stepped inside, his frame filling the doorway like a shadow swallowing the room. He didn't look angry. He looked amused. Kyle jolted backward, his breathing ragged. Aisha had never seen him look so scared. YS let his gaze sweep over the room, slow and deliberate.

"Aisha." His voice was soft, controlled.

"You really thought you could run from me?"

Aisha pressed herself against the wall, her body trembling. She had seen YS mad before. But this wasn't rage. This was something worse.

It was certainty. He knew he had already won.

His eyes flicked to Kyle.

"And you."

Kyle stiffened, his fists clenching. But Aisha saw it—the fear behind his anger.

YS smirked.

"You don't look so tough now, bruv."

Kyle flinched. The words hit like a slap.

Aisha's hands curled into fists. She knew how YS worked. He played with you first. Soft. Calm. Like he wasn't about to break you apart. YS took a slow step forward, his voice almost gentle.

"C'mon, Ai. You know how this goes. You step outta line, I gotta remind you where you belong."

Aisha's throat tightened. She had to do something. Kyle's breath was coming in short bursts. He was trembling. Not just with fear—but with anger. YS saw it too. His smirk widened. He was waiting for it.

"Look at you." YS cocked his head at Kyle.

"You're shaking, bruv."

Kyle's jaw locked. He was trying to fight it. Trying to stand his ground. But YS had already gotten inside his head. YS took another step forward, lowering his voice.

"Still a pussy."

Aisha saw it the moment Kyle snapped.

With a strangled growl, he lunged.

YS barely flinched. He was expecting it.

Sidestepping smoothly, he grabbed Kyle by the throat and slammed him back against the wall. Hard.

Aisha's heart stopped. Kyle struggled, his nails clawing at YS's grip, but it was no use. YS leaned in close, his voice a whisper.

"You forgot your place, yeah?"

Kyle gasped, his vision blurring. Not again. Not again. Aisha's pulse was a deafening roar in her ears. She had to do something. Now. Kyle's eyes locked onto hers, pleading. She had a choice. Watch him break again, or do something. Her hands curled into fists.

No. Not this time.

She lunged. Straight for YS.

Chapter 33: All or Nothing

Aisha lunged at YS with everything she had, her fists swinging wildly, her body moving on instinct. It didn't matter if she was outmatched—she refused to just stand there and let him win.

But YS barely flinched.

With terrifying ease, he caught her wrist mid-swing, his grip tightening like a vice. Aisha gasped, trying to yank free, but he didn't let go. Not this time.

"You really don't get it, do you?" YS muttered, his voice disturbingly calm.

Then he twisted her arm.

Pain shot through her shoulder as she let out a strangled cry. YS used the moment of weakness to shove her backward. Aisha hit the floor hard, the impact knocking the wind out of her. She groaned, rolling onto her side, but before she could even push herself up—

Kellie walked in.

Aisha's blood ran cold.

Kellie's slow, satisfied smirk made her stomach churn. She wasn't just here to watch. YS stepped back, stretching his fingers like nothing had happened.

"She's all yours."

Aisha's heart pounded as Kellie stalked toward her, her eyes alight with something dark and vicious. Revenge.

"What, you thought I'd forgotten?" Kellie whispered. Then she swung.

The first punch cracked against Aisha's jaw, snapping her head to the side. The second sent her sprawling onto her back. Kellie didn't stop. She rained down punches like she had been waiting her whole life for this moment.

Aisha barely had time to react. She couldn't even scream.

Kyle groaned from across the room, trying to crawl toward her, but YS's boys held him down. He struggled, but it was useless. All he could do was watch.

"You think you're special?" Kellie hissed, grabbing Aisha by the hair and yanking her up.

"You think YS ever gave a shit about you?"

Aisha's vision blurred with tears, pain flooding every inch of her body. She had nothing left.

Kellie shoved her back down, delivering a final, brutal kick to her ribs. Aisha choked on the pain, curling in on herself, shaking uncontrollably.

For a second, just a second, YS looked down at her and felt something.

Regret.

But then he remembered Shots. Darnell. The betrayal.

And just like that, regret turned to rage.

YS's chest tightened, his expression darkening as he clenched his jaw.

"Hold him down."

Kyle's stomach dropped. No. No, no, no—

"NO!" He thrashed against the hands holding him, screaming Aisha's name.

He knew what was coming. Aisha's body trembled, her mind screaming for this not to be real. This couldn't be real. One by one, YS's boys stepped forward towards Aisha. Kyle's throat was raw as he screamed for them to stop.But there was nothing he could do.

Nothing at all.

One by one, they did the unthinkable to Aisha.

Chapter 34: The Cost of Freedom

Aisha drifted in and out of consciousness, the pain anchoring her somewhere between reality and oblivion. Every inch of her body throbbed, a constant reminder of what had been taken from her. She was hollow. A body without a soul. The cold air pressed against her skin, but she barely felt it. Somewhere in the distance, she heard voices—muffled, distorted. Nothing felt real.Kyle sat on the floor nearby, his back against the wall, his knees pulled up to his chest. His head was in his hands, fingers tangled in his hair. He hadn't spoken since they left. YS was gone. His boys were gone. Kellie was gone. The nightmare was over.

But for Aisha, it would never be over.

She was drifting, but she wasn't unconscious. She was trapped inside herself. Locked away in the only safe space she could create—one where she didn't feel. Her body was broken, but that wasn't what hurt the most. It was what had been stolen from her. She tried to summon a single emotion—anger, sadness, fear. But there was nothing. Just an overwhelming emptiness that spread through her like a disease. Kyle's breath was shaky and uneven. He had spent hours trapped in his own mind, reliving it over and over again. The screams, the pleading, the laughter. The way YS had held him down, forcing him to watch.

He wanted to be sick. He wanted to tear himself apart.

Aisha shifted slightly, a soft whimper escaping her lips. Kyle's head snapped up. Guilt crushed him like a weight too heavy to bear.

"Aisha," he whispered, his voice raw.

She didn't respond. Didn't even look at him.

Kyle swallowed hard. He wanted to say something. Anything. But what could he possibly say? *Sorry?* Sorry wasn't enough. Sorry was pathetic. Aisha's gaze was fixed on nothing, her eyes dull and lifeless. She had disappeared into herself. Kyle's chest ached. He had failed her. He had failed Darnell. He had failed everyone. What kind of man was he?

A long silence stretched between them. Heavy. Suffocating.

Finally, Aisha spoke. Her voice was barely above a whisper.

"I want to die."

Kyle's stomach dropped. The words hit harder than any punch he had ever taken.

"No," he said quickly, shaking his head.

"No, don't say that."

Aisha let out a bitter laugh, but there was no humor in it.

"You think I can live after this?" Her voice cracked.

"You think any of this just goes away?"

Kyle's throat tightened. He didn't know what to say. Aisha turned her head slightly, her bruised, swollen face barely recognizable.

"I was stupid," she whispered.

"I thought I could be different. Thought I could escape."

Kyle clenched his fists. Anger surged through him—not at Aisha, but at himself. At YS. At the entire world. Tears burned in Aisha's eyes, but they never fell. She was beyond crying. Beyond feeling anything at all.

"I don't even know who I am anymore," she admitted, her voice hollow.

"I don't think I exist."

Kyle's heart twisted. This wasn't just pain. This was complete and utter destruction. Aisha squeezed her eyes shut, inhaling shakily.

"I keep thinking… if I had just died back there, it would've been easier."

Kyle flinched like he had been slapped. He couldn't breathe.

"No," he said, his voice raw.

"Aisha, you don't mean that."

She looked at him then—just for a second. And in her gaze, he saw nothing. No anger. No sadness. Just a void. Kyle's hands curled into fists. YS had taken everything from her.

"We'll figure it out," he said, though the words felt empty.

Aisha let out a slow breath.

"There's nothing left to figure out."

Kyle looked away, his jaw tight. She was right.

Everything had changed. There was no coming back from this.

But one thing was certain.

YS had to pay.

Kyle's hands shook as he stared at the ground. He had caused Darnell's death. He had let Aisha suffer. He wasn't going to let YS walk away from this. His jaw clenched. This wasn't about revenge anymore. It was about justice. About taking back whatever small shred of control they had left.

YS thought he had won.

But he had made one mistake.

He left Kyle alive.

Chapter 35: Blood for Blood

Kyle sat in the darkness, the weight of everything pressing down on him like a vice. The air in his tiny flat felt suffocating, thick with guilt, rage, and something else—a hunger for retribution. His hands shook as he scrolled through his phone. Names. Numbers. Faces from a past he had tried to leave behind. People who owed him favours. People who wouldn't ask questions.

His thumb hovered over a contact.

Do it.

Aisha's broken face flashed in his mind. The way she stared at nothing, like her soul had already left her body. Kyle squeezed his eyes shut. His breathing was shallow and ragged. He couldn't undo what had happened. But he could make sure YS never did this to anyone else. Ever.

He hit call.

A voice answered on the second ring.

"Yo?"

Kyle hesitated. This was it. Once he spoke, there was no turning back.

"I need a favour."

A pause. Then, a chuckle.

"I was wondering when you'd call."

Kyle's grip tightened around the phone. This wasn't just about revenge anymore. It was justice. Blood for blood.

YS sat in the back of his car, the engine humming softly, his fingers tapping against his thigh. The night outside was thick with cold, but he barely felt it. His mind was still burning with the aftermath of what had happened to Aisha. He should have felt victorious. He had put Darnell's little sister exactly where she belonged— broken, humiliated, completely under his control.

So why the fuck did he feel... off?

He exhaled sharply, running a hand over his face. This wasn't about her. It was about Shots. About everything Darnell had taken from him. Aisha was just collateral. A warning. A message that no one got away with crossing him. And yet, the way she had looked at him before she stopped fighting—she just lay there, lifeless—it unsettled him. He'd seen fear before. Pain. Begging. But that look? That was emptiness.

His phone buzzed. A message. A number he didn't recognise.

You made a mistake.

YS's jaw tensed. His gut told him who it was before he even checked.

Kyle.

A slow smirk stretched across his face, but it didn't quite reach his eyes. He cracked his knuckles, leaning back against the leather seat.

"Looks like someone wants to play."

He typed back.

YS: *Pull up then.*

A beat of silence. Then three dots appeared, typing... then stopped.

YS chuckled, shaking his head.

"Pussy." But even as he said it, something gnawed at him.

Kyle had been a little boy playing in a game he didn't understand when he betrayed Darnell.

But now? Now he was a man. And men who had nothing left to lose were dangerous.

Chapter 36: The Price of Revenge

Kyle sat in the dim glow of his phone screen, the weight of his decision pressing down on him like a physical force. His chest was tight, his breath shallow. He had made the call—set things in motion—but now that it was real, an unsettling feeling twisted in his gut.

Could he do this? Could he really go through with it?

Aisha's face flickered through his mind. Not the Aisha he had first met, full of defiance and fire. But the Aisha he had last seen—the one who had stopped fighting. His grip tightened around the phone. He had to do this. There was no other way.

A text popped up on his screen.

It's done. You sure about this?

Kyle stared at the message, his pulse hammering in his ears. He had made his choice. There was no turning back.

Kyle: *Yeah.*

He locked his phone, exhaling slowly. One way or another, this ended tonight.

Aisha lay curled up on the thin mattress in her care home room, staring at the wall. She barely blinked. She barely existed. The air felt thick and heavy, pressing against her chest like a weight she couldn't lift. Time had stopped moving. Or maybe she had. Her body ached, but the pain was dull—background noise to the screaming in her mind. It was the silence that scared her the most. She used to hear her own voice in her head, arguing back, fighting, telling herself to keep going. Now? There was nothing. She thought of YS, of the look in his eyes that night. He had enjoyed it. He had wanted to break her.

And he had.

Aisha squeezed her eyes shut. She wasn't Aisha anymore.

A knock at the door barely registered. Someone calling her name—probably a staff member, maybe Kellie pretending to care. She didn't care.

She should get up. She should scream. She should cry.

But what was the point? She had lost. And losing meant you didn't get back up.

YS leaned against the bar in a darkened club, the bass vibrating through his chest. The music, the drinks, the girls draped over his lap—none of it was enough to shake the feeling creeping up his spine.

Kyle's message had been playing on repeat in his head all night.

You made a mistake.

He had laughed at it at first. Kyle wasn't a threat. Kyle was a kid who had been out of the game too long, and wouldn't have the stomach to do what needed to be done. But the longer the night dragged on, the less sure he felt.

His phone buzzed.

Outside was all the message said.

YS's smirk faltered. His fingers flexed against the glass in his hand.

He glanced around. Was this a trap?

He pushed the girl off his lap, ignoring her protest, and tapped his pocket to ensure his knife was there before heading toward the exit.

The night air was sharp against his skin as he stepped into the alley behind the club. It was too quiet.

A shadow shifted in the distance.

YS rolled his shoulders, his smirk returning.

"Alright, Kyle. Let's see if you're really about it."

Chapter 37: The Showdown

Kyle's breath was steady and controlled, but his heart pounded like a war drum in his chest. His hands curled into fists at his sides as he stepped forward into the dimly lit alley. The moment had finally come. YS stood a few feet away, his stance relaxed, his smirk cocky, but there was something else there—a flicker of tension, of calculation.

"You sure you wanna do this, bruv?" YS taunted, tilting his head.

"Last time you played this game, your boy ended up dead. You really tryna go two for two?"

Kyle's jaw clenched. Darnell's name on YS's tongue sent a bolt of fury through him.

"This ain't a game," Kyle said, his voice quiet but firm.

"Not anymore."

YS chuckled, shaking his head.

"You ain't built for this. I see it in your eyes. You got that same hesitation you had when you set up Darnell."

Kyle took another step closer.

"And you got that same arrogance that made you think you could do what you did to Aisha and walk away."

YS's smirk twitched.

"That what this is about? Her? Thought you didn't even like her."

Kyle's fists tightened. This wasn't just about Aisha. It was about everything. The cycle of violence, the manipulation, the way YS had destroyed lives and walked away laughing.

"What you did to her," Kyle said, voice raw.

"Ain't ever gonna go away. I see her face every time I close my eyes. And you? You don't get to walk away from this."

YS exhaled sharply, rolling his shoulders.

"You think I ain't been in situations worse than this? Think I ain't had little boys like you try run up on man?"

Kyle didn't move.

"Yeah? And how many of them had nothing left to lose?"

The alley fell silent.

For the first time, YS's smirk faded completely. Kyle saw it—the flicker of uncertainty. Then, without warning, YS moved. Kyle had expected a punch, but it wasn't a fist that came at him—it was the cold glint of steel.

Chapter 38: Blood on the Pavement

The blade caught the dim light of the alley, flashing silver as it slashed toward Kyle. Time slowed. Instinct kicked in—Kyle jerked back, feeling the knife slice the fabric of his jacket, just missing his skin. Too close. YS didn't hesitate. He lunged again, faster this time, but Kyle was ready. He sidestepped, his hands balling into fists. No more running. No more fear. The two collided, crashing against the alley wall. Kyle swung first, his fist connecting with YS's jaw. A sickening crack.

YS stumbled but recovered quick. Too quick.

Kyle barely had time to react before YS drove his knee into his ribs, knocking the wind out of him. The pain was sharp, blinding, but Kyle pushed through it. He had no choice. YS grabbed Kyle by the collar, slamming him against the wall. His eyes were wild now—not cocky, not smug. Just furious.

"You don't get to come for me, you little snake!" YS spat, shoving the knife closer to Kyle's throat.

"You ain't built for this life!"

Kyle struggled, pushing back with everything he had. His mind flashed with images—Aisha's face, broken and empty. Darnell bleeding out. His own hands, stained with regret.

YS pressed harder.

"Should've stayed out of it."

Then, Kyle saw his opening.

With everything he had left, he rammed his knee into YS's stomach, forcing him back. Kyle didn't stop—he tackled him to the ground, knocking the knife from his grip. Now it was just them. No weapons. No boys to back him up. Just fists. Kyle rained down punches, each one fuelled by rage, guilt, and years of built-up hate.

"This is for Darnell!" A punch to the ribs.

"This is for Aisha!" A fist colliding with YS's face, sending blood spraying against the pavement.

YS coughed, trying to push Kyle off, but Kyle pinned him down. He had the upper hand. For the first time, YS looked vulnerable. Kyle grabbed the knife. He held it above YS's chest, panting. One move. One slice. And it would be over.

YS stared up at him, his bloody lips curling into a smirk.

"Go on then. Do it. Pussy!" YS screamed.

Kyle's grip tightened. His mind screamed at him to finish it. To make YS pay. But then— Aisha's voice was faint in his mind. *Kyle, you're not like him.*

His hand trembled. Was this who he was now? A murderer?

Kyle exhaled shakily and dropped the knife. It clattered against the pavement.

YS let out a weak laugh.

"Knew you didn't have it in you."

Kyle's jaw clenched.

"Nah. But they do."

YS frowned. Footsteps echoed in the alley.

A group of shadowy figures emerged from the darkness—faces YS recognised. One especially. But it couldn't be him; last YS had heard he was doing a 7-stretch at His Majesty's Pleasure for battering a fed. But here he was. Tyrone. Or Killy, as he was known on the roads. Killy was once Darnell's older and had longstanding beef with YS' brother Shots. But what was the link to Kyle? Unknown to everyone on the roads, back in the day after Darnell got killed, the police questioned Kyle about Tyrone, as they were aware he was a significant player in this county lines operation. After witnessing the police shoot and kill Darnell, Kyle did not trust the police anymore and refused to cooperate, claiming he had never heard of Tyrone. The police case against Tyrone collapsed as there was no concrete evidence to tie Tyrone to the county lines. Somehow Tyrone found out that Kyle didn't snitch and had said he owed him one. At the time, Kyle dismissed this. Until now.

YS's smirk vanished. For the first time, he looked afraid.

Kyle stood up, stepping back, watching as the men closed in.

"You ain't walking away from this one," Kyle muttered.

Then he turned, walking away, leaving YS to face his fate alone.

Chapter 39: Consequences

The air was thick with silence as Kyle walked away from the alley, his pulse pounding in his ears. His breath was ragged, his hands trembling. It was over.

He should've felt relief. He should've felt something.

But all he felt was empty.

Kyle had always thought revenge would bring him peace. That seeing YS finally get what he deserved would somehow make the weight of everything disappear. But as he stepped onto the main road, leaving behind the darkness and the echoes of the past, the weight was still there. He had won, but at what cost?

His phone buzzed in his pocket. He ignored it. There was only one place he needed to be.

Aisha sat by the window of her care home room, knees tucked against her chest, staring blankly outside. The streetlights cast long shadows against the pavement. The world kept moving. Even though hers had stopped.

She should've been asleep. But sleep never came.

Not anymore.

She didn't know how long she had been sitting there, but then her door creaked open. A staff member? Kellie? It didn't matter. She didn't care.

But then she heard his voice. Kyle.

"Aisha."

Something inside her twisted painfully. The sound of his voice made it real again. She didn't move, didn't turn to look at him. She couldn't.

"It's done," Kyle said, his voice raw.

"It's over."

Aisha swallowed hard. She should've felt something. Satisfaction. Closure. Anything. But there was just a hollow numbness in her chest.

Kyle took a hesitant step forward.

"Aisha, I need you to say something."

She finally turned to face him. His face was bruised, his knuckles torn. He looked like a man who had just walked through hell.

"You think that changes anything?" she whispered, her voice barely audible.

"You think that makes it better?"

Kyle flinched.

"I—"

"It's over, but I'm still here," Aisha cut in, her tone sharp.

"And I still have to live with it. Every fucking day."

Kyle clenched his jaw.

"I just... I thought—"

"You thought it being over would fix me?" A bitter laugh escaped her lips.

"You don't get it, Kyle. You never did."

Kyle's chest tightened. He wanted to say something to make it right. But how could he? Some things couldn't be fixed. Aisha's fingers curled into the fabric of her hoodie, gripping tightly. She wanted to scream, but the words wouldn't come.

"Every time I close my eyes, I'm back there," she muttered, barely above a whisper.

"It never goes away, Kyle. No matter how much you wanted it to."

Kyle's throat felt tight. She was right. YS was gone, but the past wasn't.

"I thought maybe... maybe you'd feel safe now," he admitted, his voice barely steady.

"Maybe I could take back what I let happen."

Aisha finally looked at him, her expression unreadable. Then, slowly, she shook her head.

"You can't rewrite history. You can't change what I am now."

With that said, a single, lonely tear dropped down Aisha's cheek. Kyle exhaled sharply. She was gone in a way he couldn't understand.A long silence stretched between them. Then, Aisha looked away.

"I need to be alone."

Kyle opened his mouth to protest, but the look in her eyes stopped him. She was already gone.

Without another word, he turned and walked away. This time, he wasn't sure if he'd ever come back.

Chapter 40: Aftermath

Kyle woke up to a dull ache in his chest, the weight of everything pressing down on him before he even opened his eyes. The world outside had changed, but inside, nothing felt different. He lay there, staring at the ceiling, his mind replaying Aisha's words over and over again.

You can't rewrite history. You can't change what I am now.

He thought what he had done would set things right. That Aisha would somehow find peace. But she hadn't. And neither had he. Something gnawed at his gut, an unease that wouldn't let him rest. He needed to see her. To talk to her again. Maybe she just needed time. Throwing on his jacket, he left his flat and headed toward the children's home. The streets were eerily quiet, the air thick and still. Too still.

Then he saw it.

A flashing blue light reflected off the pavement ahead. An ambulance. Parked outside the children's home.

Kyle's chest tightened. His pace quickened, his heart hammering as he moved toward the entrance. Something was wrong. Staff members stood outside, their faces pale, some whispering, some crying. Then he saw the paramedics. His stomach dropped. They were wheeling someone out on a stretcher.

Fuck! No!

Kyle ran forward, pushing through the small crowd, his breath coming in short gasps. Then he saw her.

Aisha.

Her skin was deathly pale, and her arms were limp at her sides. Her wrists were wrapped in bloodstained bandages.

Kyle felt like the ground beneath him had disappeared.

"Aisha!"

Her eyes fluttered at the sound of his voice. Slowly, weakly, she turned her head toward him. Their eyes met. For one fleeting second, there was recognition. Then, she closed them again.

Kyle felt something inside him shatter.

"No, no, no—stay with me!" His voice cracked as he tried to follow, but a paramedic blocked him.

"She's unconscious. We need to get her to the hospital."

Kyle shook his head.

"I need to go with her. Please."

The paramedic hesitated, then nodded.

"Get in."

Kyle climbed into the ambulance and barged past the member of staff from the care home, grabbing Aisha's hand. It was cold. Too cold.

"You're not leaving me too," he whispered, his voice breaking.

"I won't let you."

The ambulance doors slammed shut, the siren wailing as they sped off into the distance.

Chapter 41: The Edge

YS woke up to darkness.

Pain exploded through his body the moment he tried to move. A deep, searing ache that told him he had been beaten within an inch of his life. It felt like he'd been hit by a freight train. His breathing was shallow, every inhale sending sharp stabs through his ribs. His head pounded, a deep, nauseating throb that made it hard to think.

Where the fuck was he?

Slowly, his eyes adjusted to the dim light. The scent of damp concrete and rust filled his nostrils. He could hear the slow, rhythmic drip of water somewhere nearby. An abandoned building? A warehouse? The last thing he remembered was getting rushed. Killy and his boys coming out of nowhere, fists and boots raining down on him. Then being bundled into the back of a van. After that?

Blackness.

He wasn't sure how long he had been here. Hours? Days? His mouth was dry, his stomach a hollow pit of nausea. He was weak. Vulnerable.

And worst of all—he had no control.

YS tried to move, but his wrists were bound behind him, the rough rope biting into his skin. He shifted slightly and felt something wet on his cheek. Blood. His blood. Panic clawed at his chest, but he forced himself to breathe. Panicking wouldn't help. Thinking would. He was YS.

Young Shots. The name carried weight. Respect. Fear. No one would dare—

Except they had.

And that terrified him.

A noise. A door creaking open.

YS tensed, straining to listen. Footsteps, slow and deliberate, echoed against the concrete floor. A shadow moved into view. Someone crouched in front of him, their face just out of reach of the faint light. Watching him. Studying him. YS swallowed hard, masking the fear creeping up his throat.

"If you're gonna kill me, just fucking hurry up and do it," he muttered, his voice hoarse.

A low chuckle. Then a voice, smooth and deliberate.

"Who said anything about killing you?"

A shiver ran down YS's spine. Killy then turned and walked out as quietly as he had entered.

For the first time in his life, YS felt powerless.

Chapter 42: The Waiting Room

The hospital waiting room was a blur of white lights and antiseptic silence. Kyle sat in a rigid plastic chair, elbows on his knees, hands knotted together so tightly they had turned white. Time didn't feel real. Minutes dragged like hours. Every second felt like a countdown to something he couldn't name. A nurse had told him they'd pumped Aisha's stomach. That she was stable—for now. But the words felt hollow. Mechanical. Like they were words from a script.

He had never felt so powerless.

Kyle looked down at his hands, still stained faintly with blood. Aisha's blood. He squeezed his eyes shut, trying to block out the image of her pale face, her limp body, the way she looked at him before she closed her eyes.

She had given up.

And he had let her.

The door behind him opened, and Kyle's head jerked up. A nurse stepped out, her face unreadable.

"She's in ICU. We've pumped her stomach, we've managed to stabilise her heart rate and stop the bleeding. But she's not conscious yet."

"Can I see her?" he asked, voice hoarse.

The nurse hesitated, then nodded.

"Just for a minute."

Kyle followed her down a long corridor. The hum of machines and muffled voices filled the air, but all he could hear was his own heartbeat. She was in the corner room. When the nurse opened the door, Kyle almost couldn't walk in. Aisha looked so small. So fragile. Her arms were bandaged. Tubes running from her arms. Machines beeped in a rhythm that felt both reassuring and terrifying. He sat down beside her and reached out, brushing his fingers against hers.

"You said I couldn't fix this," he whispered.

"But I'm still here. And I'm not leaving."

Her chest rose and fell, steady but shallow. No flicker of her eyes. No sign she heard him.

"You were right, Aish. Trying to take care of YS didn't fix you. Or me. But maybe... maybe this can."

He paused, swallowing hard.

"Please. Just give me the chance. Let me prove to you that life's still worth something. That *you're* still worth everything."

He lowered his head beside her hand, eyes burning. And in the silence of the ICU, Kyle kept holding on.

Chapter 43: The Fall of YS

YS was drifting in and out of consciousness, and each time he came to, it was worse. His body throbbed in places he could no longer distinguish. One of his eyes was swollen completely shut. His jaw clicked painfully when he swallowed. There was blood on his lips, his chest, and the concrete floor around him. Dried and flaking. Fresh and hot. He had lost track of time. The warehouse had become his tomb. No sunlight. No sound but the occasional rat scuttling or dripping water. And the door. That damned metal door that groaned open when they came to hurt him, question him, and break him.

But they hadn't come in a while.

That was the part he hated most now.

The silence.

Because in the silence, he had to sit with his thoughts. He tried to remember how long he'd been here. His mind fractured every time he tried. Time didn't exist here—

only pain. And regret. His pride had always been his armour. But now it was brittle, crumbling. And underneath it was fear. He remembered the look in Aisha's eyes when she'd started to pull away. Not fear. Not even hate. Something worse.

Disgust.

He remembered how Kyle looked at him—not with respect, not with intimidation—but with pity. That had rattled him more than he wanted to admit. What did he have left now? The name "Young Shots" used to mean something. Power. Respect. Fear. But none of that mattered when you were tied to a chair, piss-soaked, beaten until the breath left your lungs, and no one was coming for you. He wasn't sure when he started crying. But he knew when he stopped—when the door creaked open again.

Footsteps.

He tensed, trying to sit up, but pain screamed through his side. A rib cracked. Or maybe it had already been cracked days ago. He didn't know anymore.

"Still alive, then," someone said. A voice he recognised. Killy.

YS turned his head slowly. His mouth was dry. He could barely speak.

"What... what do you want?"

Killy stepped into view, crouching beside him.

"Same thing we've always wanted, YS. Answers. Names. A little bit of repentance."

YS laughed, a broken, bitter sound.

"Fuck you."

But there was no conviction in it. He wasn't YS anymore. Not really. Killy leaned closer.

"You keep acting like this ends on your terms. It doesn't. You ended a lot of people's stories. Now we're writing yours."

There was something in Killy's eyes. Not rage. Not satisfaction.

Pity.

And that hurt more than the beatings.

When the door slammed shut again, YS let his head fall back against the concrete, a low, broken whimper escaping his throat. He was beginning to understand what real fear was. Not the fear of pain. The fear of *oblivion*. The fear that nothing he'd done would mean anything now. That he'd vanish in the dark, like he'd never existed.

He had ruled like a king.

And now he was dying like a dog.

And worse—he knew he deserved it.

Chapter 44: Holding On

The ICU was colder that morning. Or maybe it was Kyle's nerves making it feel that way. He hadn't slept. Not really. Just slumped forward in the chair, eyes flickering open every few minutes to check Aisha's breathing. Every shallow rise and fall of her chest was a small lifeline he refused to let go of.

He'd held her hand through the night. Kept whispering to her in the silence, even though she didn't respond. Part of him believed she could hear him. Part of him was terrified she couldn't.

The nurses came and went like ghosts—efficient, gentle, and kind. Their movements were rehearsed, their smiles soft, but their eyes... their eyes held the weight of experience. They had seen too many girls like Aisha. Girls who had been discarded, broken by the world, and barely stitched back together.

Kyle had learned to read those looks. They were all waiting. Watching. Preparing for the worst.

He hated how pale Aisha looked. How still. The girl he'd once known was loud, bold, and sharp with her tongue. Even when she'd been hurting, she carried it with fire. Now, she was barely there.

He leaned in closer, brushing her hair gently back from her face.

"You don't get to go like this, Aish. Not after everything. Not after surviving hell."

His throat tightened. His voice cracked.

"You think this world broke you? It didn't. You're still here. And I'm still here. I'm not leaving. Not again."

His memories blurred together—Aisha laughing, Aisha angry, Aisha screaming at him for taking her brother away. He had failed her in every possible way. But this time, he was going to stay.

"If you wanna scream at me, hate me, never forgive me—that's fine. I'll take it. I deserve it. But please... just give me the chance to make it right. Please."

He lowered his head beside her hand, resting his forehead against her skin. It was warm—but fragile. Too fragile.

"You matter, Aisha," he whispered.

"More than you know. You always did. Even when the world tried to convince you otherwise."

He paused. His breath hitched.

"I'm sorry for every time I wasn't there. For every time I let you believe you were alone. You never were. Not really. And you're not now."

A long moment passed. Nothing. Just the rhythm of the machines.

Then—a flicker on the monitor. A faint but unmistakable spike.

Kyle's head snapped up.

Aisha's fingers twitched.

He jolted upright.

"Nurse! Somebody! She moved—she moved!"

Chaos erupted around him. Nurses rushing in, footsteps and instructions blending into a blur. Kyle stepped back, heart in his throat, unable to take his eyes off her.

Aisha's eyelids fluttered. Her head shifted slightly on the pillow.

"Aisha?" Kyle said, trembling.

Her eyes opened. Slowly. Blinking. Unfocused at first—then searching.

Her gaze found him.

"Kyle," she rasped. Barely audible. Fragile.

He choked back a sob, nodding, clutching her hand.

"I'm here. I'm not going anywhere."

A tear slid down her cheek.

And Kyle—who had seen death, betrayal, and pain—felt something crack open inside him.

Hope.

They weren't out of the woods. But for the first time in a long time... they were holding on.

Chapter 45: Cracks Beneath the Surface

The room was muted, heavy with the rhythmic beeping of machines. Aisha lay still, but inside her mind, a storm was raging.

She was aware, faintly, of the presence beside her. Warm fingers clutching her hand. A voice whispering in the dark. Kyle. Always, Kyle.

Part of her wanted to pull away. She didn't deserve saving. She didn't deserve softness.
Another part—the part she thought had long since died—wanted to grip his hand back and never let go.

Why won't you leave me alone? She thought bitterly, even as her fingers twitched instinctively toward him.

Pain lanced through her body, but it was nothing compared to the weight crushing her chest. The guilt. The shame. The endless question of why she had survived when it would've been easier not to.

She hated herself for wanting him there. Hated herself even more for needing it.

Kyle's voice broke through the fog again. Pleading. Desperate. Promising things he couldn't possibly fix.

He doesn't understand, she thought. *He thinks this is something you can patch up with words.*

She wasn't broken. She was *ruined.*

Tears burned behind her eyes, but she refused to let them fall. She had cried enough. Enough for her mother. For Darnell. For the girl she used to be.

Kyle's forehead rested against her hand, his body trembling slightly. She felt the desperation pouring off him, and it both comforted and terrified her.

I can't be saved, she thought. *Not really. And if he tries... he's just going to drown with me.*

Aisha forced her heavy eyelids open. The effort was monumental. Every muscle screamed in protest.

The first thing she saw was him. Kyle. His face was gaunt with sleepless nights, his eyes red and raw with grief.

"Kyle," she rasped, her voice barely more than a broken breath.

The way he reacted—like the sound of her voice was oxygen—shattered something deep inside her.

He wasn't faking it. He wasn't pretending.

He still cared. Even after everything. And that was the most terrifying thing of all. A tear slid down her cheek—not from weakness, but from a grief so old and deep that it had no name anymore.

Kyle gripped her hand tighter, as if trying to anchor her to the earth.

"I'm here," he whispered fiercely.

"I'm not going anywhere."

Aisha closed her eyes again, exhausted by the simple act of existing. But for the first time, she didn't slip into darkness alone. Kyle was there. And somewhere deep inside the battered ruins of her heart... a small, cautious spark flared back to life.

The air in the ICU felt heavier now, thick with unspoken words. Kyle squeezed Aisha's hand gently, feeling how fragile she was beneath his touch, terrified that if he gripped too hard, she might slip away again. Aisha's eyes fluttered open, still glazed with exhaustion. She shifted slightly against the pillow, her throat working as she struggled to speak.

Kyle leaned closer, his heart thudding painfully.

"Take your time, Aish. I'm not going anywhere."

Her lips parted. No words came at first. Only a breath, shaky and uncertain.

Inside her mind, the battle raged.

Say something. Anything. Let him know you're still here.

But every time she tried, the weight of everything she'd endured choked her silent.

She looked at him—really looked at him. His face was battered, worn, and haunted by guilt and hope all at once. She wanted to tell him how angry she was. How broken she felt. How part of her blamed him, and another part clung to him like a drowning girl to a raft.

But the words wouldn't come.

Tears blurred her vision. Her body ached, her mind screamed, and yet... somehow, Kyle's presence steadied her. Kept her anchored to this world she wasn't sure she wanted anymore.

Finally, her voice cracked out, raw and almost inaudible:

"Why didn't you let me go?"

Kyle's breath hitched sharply. He shook his head, gripping her hand tighter, his own tears slipping free.

"Because you're not meant to leave yet," he whispered fiercely.

"Because you've still got a life worth living. Even if you can't see it yet, I can."

Aisha closed her eyes, feeling the hot sting of tears leak down her temples.

I don't believe you.
I want to believe you.
I'm scared to believe you.

She had spent so long fighting, surviving, and enduring. And now the idea of hope—of trusting someone again—felt terrifying. Almost worse than all the pain.

"I'm tired, Kyle," she whispered.

"So tired."

"I know," he said, pressing his forehead against the back of her hand.

"I know you are. So rest. Just... don't give up yet."

Aisha drifted back into sleep, his words wrapping around her like a threadbare blanket.
Not forgiveness. Not trust. Not yet.

But something.

Something that might, one day, be enough.

Chapter 46: In the Dark

YS drifted in and out of consciousness, his mind trapped somewhere between delirium and nightmare.

Every part of him hurt—deep, gnawing pain that never let up. His mouth was so dry he could barely move his tongue. His wrists were shredded raw from the rope. His clothes were stiff with blood, sweat, and filth.

But it wasn't the physical pain that broke him.

It was the silence.

The unbearable quiet of being left alone with nothing but his thoughts—his mistakes—his regrets.

He had always thought he'd die in a blaze of glory. Shot in a standoff. Rushed by rivals. Something fast.

Something loud. Something fitting for a name like Young Shots.

But this?

This slow, rotting, forgotten death?

It terrified him in a way he didn't know was possible.

Footsteps echoed in the distance, dragging him from the edge of unconsciousness. He struggled to lift his head, the movement sending white-hot agony through his body.

A shadow loomed over him.

Killy.

And someone else this time. Another man—older, colder. Someone YS didn't recognize. Someone who didn't care who he was—or who he had been.

Killy crouched down, smiling a humourless smile.

"Still breathing, huh?" Killy said lightly, as if he was commenting on the weather.

"Strong little fucker."

YS tried to speak, but only a hoarse croak escaped.

The older man knelt down, setting a small black case beside him. He opened it slowly, methodically.

YS caught a glimpse of what was inside—and his blood ran cold.

Blades. Pliers. Tools are meant for breaking, not fixing.

Panic clawed at him, desperate and wild. He tried to twist away, but there was nowhere to go. No escape.

Killy leaned in, voice low and almost gentle.

"Remember all them kids you ruined? All the lives you wrecked? This... this is justice."

YS opened his mouth to beg—to lie—to promise anything—but the older man pressed a hand to his chest, pinning him down effortlessly.

"You ain't dying yet," Killy said softly.

"Not until you feel every single thing you made others feel."

YS's heart pounded so hard he thought it might explode. His body shook with terror.

For the first time since he was twelve years old, since Shots had been taken away, YS prayed.

But no one was listening.

And the darkness closed in again.

Chapter 47: Broken Bargains

Pain flared through YS's body with every shallow breath. His mind reeled, struggling to stay conscious. Every nerve ending screamed. Every heartbeat was agony. Through the haze of pain, he heard Killy's voice, cold and measured.

"You think this is just payback?" Killy said, pacing slowly in front of him.

"You think this is just about what you did to those kids?"

YS coughed, blood trickling from the corner of his mouth. He barely had the strength to lift his head.

"It's bigger than that," Killy continued.

"You built an empire off the backs of kids like Aisha. Like my cousin. Like the ones you left dead in alleyways."

YS tried to sneer, tried to summon some shred of his old bravado, but it was gone. Stripped away piece by piece.

"And now," Killy said, stopping right in front of him,

"you're gonna make it right."

The older man—the one with the black case—knelt down again, wordless, clinical. The glint of steel made YS's stomach twist. Killy crouched to YS's level, his voice dropping to a whisper filled with ice.

"I want names. Connects. Drop spots. Every little dirty secret you've got buried under that fake swagger of yours."

YS's chest heaved. He shook his head weakly.

"You... you're just... another snake..."

Killy smiled, almost pityingly.

"Maybe," he said.

"But at least I know who I am."

He leaned in closer. YS could smell the stale cigarette smoke on his breath.

"And you? You're nothing. Just a scared little boy who thought running dope made him invincible."

YS's heart pounded. He knew how this worked. If he gave up the information, maybe—*maybe*—they'd kill him quicker.

If he didn't? He'd wish he had.

He squeezed his eyes shut. He tried to conjure up the memory of who he used to be. The boy who stood tall in the streets. The boy who didn't flinch. But all he could see now were the faces of the kids he'd destroyed.

Aisha's eyes. Betrayed. Broken.

The knife-edge of panic carved through him.

"You got one chance," Killy said, voice razor-sharp.

"Start talking. Or we'll start cutting."

YS let out a ragged breath.

He knew what they wanted. He knew he couldn't hold out forever. And for the first time in his short, brutal life, YS was genuinely, soul-deep afraid.

Chapter 48: Ghosts in Her Blood

The days blurred. Machines beeped. Nurses whispered. Aisha slept.

But not peacefully.

When the painkillers wore off, her body screamed. Not just with pain—but memory. Her nerves flinched at every noise, every shadow. Her chest tightened when someone touched her too quickly. Even kindness hurts now.

Her veins burned. Her mouth tasted of metal and shame. The doctors said she was lucky. Kyle said he was proud. The staff at the care home offered tight-lipped smiles and practiced encouragement.

But Aisha didn't feel lucky.

She felt haunted.

Every time she closed her eyes, she saw flashes. The warehouse. The laughter as fists rained down. Kellie's face twisted with jealousy. Shante's boot cracking her ribs. YS's voice in her ear—seductive, convincing, venomous.

Family, he'd whispered once. *Loyalty.*

Now the words made her want to retch.

Her fingers twitched at night, instinctively searching for the burner phone she no longer had. For the joint that dulled her edges. For the voice that promised her belonging and delivered hell. Sometimes she woke up gasping, drenched in sweat, clutching her stomach as if she could claw the memories out. Other times, she didn't want to wake up at all.

Kyle came every day. Same hoodie. Same tired eyes. He looked like guilt had taken root in his bones and wouldn't let go. He brought her magazines. Whispered jokes. Told stories about Darnell when they were kids. He tried to remind her that she was more than what had been done to her. Sometimes, she laughed. But it always felt wrong. Like her mouth didn't remember how. She didn't know how to be in this body anymore. Didn't know how to be a girl who had survived the kind of pain no one should. She felt like a ghost of herself—like something had been hollowed out inside her and filled with tar.

She stared at the ceiling a lot. Counted tiles. Counted seconds between beeps. Counted all the ways she could leave again.

The blade. The pills. The silence.

But she remembered Kyle's face. The way he'd looked at her in the ambulance—like she was worth saving. Like she was still someone.

It made her feel something.

And that terrified her more than the pain.

One night, long after visiting hours, she whispered into the dark:

"I don't know who I am without the pain."

Kyle, half-asleep in the chair beside her, stirred. He blinked, leaned forward, eyes red and heavy.

"Then we'll find out together," he said, his voice rough with emotion.

And for the first time, Aisha believed he meant it.

Even if she didn't know how.

Chapter 49: Lines Still Crossed

Aisha had been home for three days. Or rather, she'd been back in the care system. The home was different now—new staff, new girls, but the same tired walls and the same dead eyes.

Everyone walked around like ghosts, going through routines with forced smiles and eyes that said, *don't get too close.*

Kyle visited when he could, but it wasn't the same. There was distance now, not just physical—emotional. Like a gap had opened between them, and neither of them knew how to cross it.

Aisha felt like she was slipping again. Her progress was surface-deep, brittle, like glass stretched too thin. Every night, the walls seemed to press in closer. The other girls whispered behind closed doors and laughed at things Aisha didn't understand. She felt out of place. Out of time. Like she was watching her own life through a pane of glass, unable to touch it. She told herself she was getting better. That surviving meant something. But every night, she stared at the ceiling, feeling the weight of everything she couldn't say out loud. That she didn't feel safe. That she didn't feel clean. That she didn't know who she was outside of pain. That every time she smiled, it felt like a betrayal to the broken girl inside her.

And so, one morning, before the sun had fully risen, Aisha packed what little she had and walked out of the care home. No noise. No warning. Just silence.

When Kyle arrived later that morning, her bed was stripped bare. Her toothbrush gone. Her notebook is missing.

All that remained was a folded piece of paper under her pillow.

> *Thank you for seeing me. But I need to figure out who I am without anyone else's eyes on me. Don't come looking.*

He stared at it for what felt like hours. The words blurred. The meaning didn't.

She was gone.

He slumped into the chair beside her empty bed, burying his face in his hands. The guilt crawled back up his throat like bile. But beneath it was something worse—

Understanding.

Because if he were her, he might have run too.

Chapter 50: Missing Pieces

The warehouse reeked of rust, blood, and something sour—like rot.

Blood stained the floor. Rope scraps littered the ground. The chair YS had been tied to was overturned. Empty.

Gone.

Killy stood in the doorway, fists clenched so tight his knuckles turned bone white.

"We thought he was dead," one of his boys muttered from behind, pacing.

Killy didn't speak. His jaw worked as he stared at the blood. At the remnants of everything they thought they'd buried.

He had planned it meticulously—down to the last hour. No mercy. No forgiveness. But now? Now it was chaos. Someone had to have intervened. Someone who had reason to want YS breathing.

He crouched beside the ropes, touching the frayed ends.

"Someone came for him," he said finally. His voice was low, steady, and furious.

"Someone still loyal. Or someone who wants what he knows."

The room fell silent.

He rose slowly, eyes narrowing. The streets would feel this. Every crew. Every runner. Every girl caught in between.

YS had vanished.

And the streets were already whispering.

Final Chapter: A Message

Aisha sat on a weather-beaten bench at the edge of a city she didn't know. The air was cold. Her coat is too big. Her hood was pulled low. Everything about her said, *don't notice me.*

She watched people pass—couples laughing, parents yelling at their kids, runners on phones. Normal. Untouchable. Free.

She was miles away from the girl in that ICU bed. But every step forward still felt like walking through mud.

The burner phone she bought when she left buzzed in her pocket. A sound she hadn't heard in weeks. A sound that made her stomach twist instantly.

She pulled it out slowly, heart racing, fingertips numb.

She didn't recognise the number.

She opened the message.

> "Miss me?" You should've stayed gone."

For a moment, she didn't move. She just stared at the screen as if her breath had frozen in her chest.

The world didn't stop. No one around her knew. But inside Aisha, everything shifted.

She locked the phone slowly, placed it in her coat pocket, and looked out across the street. The cold bit at her skin. Her pulse thundered in her ears.

She wasn't scared.

She was angry.

And this time, she wouldn't run.

To be continued...

Printed in Dunstable, United Kingdom